THE LEFT-OUTS

Joan is certainly in a mess. People make fun of her weight, her parents have split up, and even school is no escape. Used to being popular, it hurts to find she can't impress her new teacher, or classmates. Then the final humiliation, she fails to gain a speaking part in the form play, The Pied Piper, and is cast as a rat, alone with eight other class mates.

But Joan is a fighter, and soon the rats have formed a secret club – The Left-Outs. With Joan as leader of the gang, they have special rules and badges, and swear to stick up for each other against the rest of the world. They also begin rehearsals for a brilliant play of their own – and the results surprise even Joan herself.

Born in 1945, Jacqueline Wilson has twice been short-listed for the Observer Teenage Fiction Award. She lives in Kingston-upon-Thames and this is her first book in Puffin.

The LEFT-OUTS

Jacqueline Wilson

OOKS

and Son Limited

PUFFIN BOOKS

Published by the Penguin Group
Penguin Books Ltd, 27 Wrights Lane, London W8 5TZ, England
Viking Penguin, a division of Penguin Books USA Inc.
375 Hudson Street, New York, New York 10014, USA
Penguin Books Australia Ltd, Ringwood, Victoria, Australia
Penguin Books Canada Ltd, 2801 John Street, Markham, Ontario, Canada L3R 1B4
Penguin Books (NZ) Ltd, 182–190 Wairau Road, Auckland 10, New Zealand

Penguin Books Ltd, Registered Offices: Harmondsworth, Middlesex, England

First published by Blackie and Son Limited 1989
Published in Puffin Books 1991
1 3 5 7 9 10 8 6 4 2

One

It's six o'clock on Sunday morning but Joan's already up. She's sitting cross-legged on the floor in her Batman pyjamas, trying to make a Plasticine lavatory. Not a life-size lavatory, of course. She's trying to make a tiny model of Dad's new flat in a shoebox. She's already made a big blue bed for Dad and a little blue bed for herself, a yellow table and two chairs, a soft green sofa with separate Plasticine cushions and a red television and video and cassette recorder.

She's remembered a kettle and a gadget for making toasted sandwiches (in the grey sludge that comes when you mix all the Plasticine colours together) but she's not bothering with a proper kitchen. They can always have take-aways. Joan imagines her future meals. Day after day of hamburgers and hot dogs, fish and chips and pizzas, sweet and sour pork and beef curry, Kentucky chicken and chocolate chip cookies, prawn cocktail crisps and cans of Coke, strawberry ice-cream and giant Mars Bars. She licks her lips at the thought.

So they don't need a kitchen but they do need a bathroom. She's made the bath already, a very stylish green affair. (The same green as the sofa,

5

and if Joan shakes the shoebox she might have difficulty sorting out sofa from bath). She's made a big bottle of bubble bath too. And now she's doing her best with the lavatory.

It's proving quite a hard job. She tries to make a chain but it keeps getting too thin and breaking. The lavatory will have to have a handle instead. She's not quite sure where it goes. She's used a lavatory every day of her life (apart from her first year or two in nappies) but she's never really given one a searching look to see how it's designed.

She leaves her shoebox flat for a moment and patters off in her bare feet to investigate their own lavatory. She doesn't think much of it. She doesn't like anything about this new flat of theirs. That's why she's so thrilled that Dad is moving out of that little rented room and getting a proper flat of his own. A flat big enough for Joan to come too. She's got it all sorted out in her mind. Of course she'll miss Mum at first. But Mum's got Jackie, Joan's sister. Joan feels she won't miss Jackie one little bit.

Joan looks carefully at the lavatory. She notices for the first time that there's a lid on top of the cistern. She prises it off and has a look inside. There's a big orange ball bobbing on top of the water. Joan has a go at flushing the lavatory and sees what happens inside the cistern. It's quite interesting. She waits and then has another go. And another. She tries fiddling around with the orange ball and the bits it's attached to, just to see if it makes any difference. It does. There's a sudden snap and a part comes away in Joan's hand. The

6

water bubbles ominously.

'Oh, help,' Joan whispers, and hurriedly drops the broken bit back inside the cistern. She crams on the lid. Maybe the bit will somehow nudge itself back into the right place. Maybe.

Joan runs rather rapidly back to her bedroom. She bangs the door behind her in her haste and Jackie peers out from under her duvet.

'Why are you running a four-minute mile through our bedroom?' she says, crossly.

'Mmm? I'm not running,' says Joan, breathing heavily, crouching down in front of her shoebox.

'And you're playing with that mucky Plasticine again. I just hate that smell.'

'I hate all your smells,' says Joan, putting the finishing touches to the Plasticine lavatory.

'I *don't* smell!' Jackie says, indignantly.

'Yes, you do,' says Joan, putting the lavatory in place and starting to make a little plasticine model of Dad. 'You smell positively disgusting. All those different perfumes and your hair stuff and that hand lotion and what about your nail varnish? It's a wonder I don't expire on the spot, having to breathe in all your dangerous polluting muck.'

'Yes, *about* my nail varnish, Joan. What's happened to my Flame Red, eh? I only bought it from Boots on Friday and yet half the bottle's gone already.'

'I don't see why you're accusing me,' says Joan, lovingly fashioning Dad a new blue suit. She waves her Plasticiney fingers in the air, showing off her bare, bitten nails.

7

'I know you haven't put it on your stubby little fingers. But you've used it for something else, I bet. I know you,' says Jackie, sitting up in bed and glaring at her sister.

'You're always getting at me,' says Joan, looking wounded. Although in actual fact she did use just a little of the Flame Red. She made a Plasticine hospital on Saturday morning, when Mum and Jackie were out shopping. Red Plasticine was a bit too solid and lumpy for blood. Flame Red nail varnish was much more effective. Joan also borrowed Jackie's Purple Haze eyeshadow to make the patients look suitably haggard, and her black Kohl eyeliner came in useful for several sad cases of gangrene. Jackie might get even crosser when she examines the contents of her make-up bag, but Joan decides she'll maintain total innocence as long as it is practical.

Jackie gets cross enough when she glances at her alarm clock.

'It's twenty past *six!*' she squeaks. 'Why are you up at this time, you idio

'It's Sunday,' says J   We're seeing Dad today.' She gives the   ne Dad a fond pat, and then start   erself.

'Oh, big deal,'

She doesn't s   he and Mum sp

'He's no

'I kno

lump

Mu

to go on a diet. Dad says she's just cuddly. Jackie says she's a Large Fat Lump. The children at this new school started to call her Fatso, but Joan retaliated with her own self-taught version of Karate and that's subdued them a little.

Joan makes red sausage arms and legs for the Plasticine Joan and then waggles them violently in the air, karate chopping a host of invisible enemies. Then she sits her on the sofa in the shoebox, next to Dad.

Five and a half days seem to go past, instead of five and a half hours. But Dad arrives at last and Joan gives him a big hug and kiss. Jackie hangs back and greets him with a cool hello. Mum barely manages that. She's busy on the phone, trying to track down a plumber willing to come out on a Sunday.

'A plumber?' says Dad, ruffling Joan's hair.

'Yes, a plumber. The loo's been overflowing all morning. Goodness knows what's wrong with it,' Mum says, sighing.

'Why don't you ask Dad to fix it, Mum?' Joan suggests, hastily.

'Because your Dad always makes a botch of things,' says Mum. 'Just mind your own business, Joan.'

Joan sighs and decides she maybe won't miss Mum quite so much after all. She wonders how long it will be before she can move in with Dad. It will be absolutely great if he says she can move in right away.

'Can we see the new flat, Dad?' she asks, as soon

as they're in the car.

Joan is sitting in the front with Dad. Jackie lounges in the back seat, flicking through her love comic.

'Yes, of course you can see the flat. I thought we'd have tea there. But it's a lovely day. Let's eat out, have a walk in the park and go to the children's zoo first.'

Jackie groans.

'What's the matter, Jackie?' Dad asks.

'Nothing.'

'Take no notice of her,' says Joan. 'She's just fed up because she went to this Under 16s disco last night and this drippy boy she fancies didn't dance with her.'

'You shut up,' says Jackie, furiously. 'You don't know anything about it.'

'Yes, I do. I heard you on the phone to your stupid friends, going on and on about Mick, and how you hoped you'd get off with him. And then this morning—'

'You're just a nasty little eavesdropper,' says Jackie, smacking at Joan's head with her magazine.

'Girls, girls!' says Dad. 'Joan! Stop that!'

She's halfway over the back of her seat, attempting to retaliate.

'Where do you want to have lunch?' he says, craftily.

Joan knows he's trying to distract her—but it works all the same. She calms down and starts a serious discussion about food. Dad thinks hard and take them to a pub in Chelsea for a treat. There's a special dining area where children are allowed. Dad settles them at a table and asks what they'd like to drink.

'Bacardi and Coke please,' says Joan, with an air of sophistication.

She gets the Coke. Jackie has a Perrier water, because she's watching her weight, although she's half Joan's size. Joan isn't watching her weight at all. She has roast duck with orange sauce, roast potatoes and mixed vegetables and then she has chocolate fudge cake with cream for pudding. She eats every mouthful with appreciation.

'You make me feel sick just watching you,' says Jackie, daintily nibbling her salad.

'Don't you girls ever stop getting at each other?' says Dad, wearily.

'We're totally incompatible,' says Joan. 'And it's got much worse since we had to sell our old house and live in this horrible poky flat.'

Dad sighs. 'Now Joan—'

'You've no idea how awful it is having to share a bedroom with her,' says Jackie. 'It's ridiculous. Now I'm fourteen and practically grown up, I ought to have a bit of privacy.'

'Yes, so really it would make much more sense if—if we were separated,' says Joan, delicately. She takes a deep breath. She's about to ask Dad if she can come and live with him right away but he gets in first.

'Well, you're actually both agreeing at the moment! Let's drink to that. Another Perrier, Jackie? A Coke, Joan?'

'Yes, please, but Dad—'

'In a minute.'

Try as she might, she can't get him back to the subject. They walk over Albert Bridge to Battersea Park and stroll round the gardens. Joan hangs on Dad's arm. Jackie hobbles behind them in her new high heels, complaining about the gravel paths and the soft grass.

They go to the free children's zoo and Joan says hello to all her favourites, the sleepy owl-monkey, the wicked-looking goats, the lemurs holding their tails high in the air, and best of all, the black apes with the rude red bottoms.

'Trust you to like them best,' says Jackie.

They go to the little zoo shop too and Joan talks Dad into buying her another pack of Plasticine. She's also very keen on a long wiggly rubber snake but Dad is too sensible to buy it for her.

'What about you, Jackie? Do you fancy anything?' Dad offers.

'I don't play with *toys,* Dad,' says Jackie, scornfully.

'Yes, like Jackie said, she's nearly grown up now,' says Joan. 'She and Mum have got ever so close. You should just hear them nattering on about men and make-up and clothes and that. It gets so boring for me, Dad. I feel really left out at times. I wish I didn't have to be stuck with them. It would be great if I could move out altogether. You know. Go and live with someone else.'

Dad sighs and tries hard to change the subject. Joan is relentless. They walk back for the car.

'Are you taking us to your new flat now, Dad?' she asks excitedly. 'I can't wait to see what it's like. Don't worry if you haven't got it all sorted out yet. You need someone to give you a hand, help make it really cosy. I could help if you like, Dad. In fact . . . I could come and stay now, couldn't I?'

Dad swallows hard. He keeps his eyes fixed on the road ahead as he drives.

'Oh, Joan. Look, I know you've been hinting about it all day. And of course I'd *love* you to come and live with me—you too, Jackie— but I'm afraid it's not possible at the moment.'

'Yes, it is!' says Joan. 'Never mind about Jackie, she's fine with Mum. But I can come. You kept saying when you had that rented room that I had to wait till you got a proper place of your own. And now you have.'

'Yes, but it's a little matchbox of a flat. With only one bedroom.'

'Well, I don't mind sharing,' says Joan. 'Or I could have a camp bed in the living room if you like. I'm not fussy. But you need someone to look after you, Dad, to do your washing and cleaning and all that.'

'And you're volunteering, Joan?' says Jackie, spluttering in the back seat. 'You've never washed so much as a pair of socks yourself. And the one time you tried to use the vacuum cleaner you pressed the wrong switch and sprayed the entire contents of the dust bag all over the carpet.'

'Take no notice of her, Dad. She always tries to put me down. We could go to the Launderette—

and what does it matter about a bit of dust?'

'I'm sure you'd look after me splendidly, Joan,' says Dad. 'But the thing is . . . well, I've got somebody else to look after me now.'

'What?' says Joan.

'You see, I've met this very lovely lady, Lizzie—'

'There! Mum knew you had a girlfriend,' says Jackie.

Joan says nothing at all. Dad reaches out and tries to take Joan's hand. Joan snatches it away.

'I know you'll like Lizzie when you meet her,' says Dad.

Joan hates Lizzie. She's young and skinny, in tight jeans and a stripy T shirt. She's got frizzy hair tied with a baby ribbon. She does her best to make friends but Joan still says nothing at all, and Jackie says very little. Lizzie has made a big tea, and she's included all Joan's favourites: trifle and chocolate eclairs and cream doughnuts, things Mum won't ever let her eat.

But Joan eats nothing. She doesn't even touch the doughnut Dad puts on her plate.

'Oh, well. She had a very big lunch,' says Dad, apologetically.

Jackie eats half a sandwich precisely.

Lizzie doesn't seem very hungry herself, but Dad pretends to be ravenous and eats enormously. He doesn't look as if he's enjoying it though.

'Well. That was a really lovely tea,' he says, and he smiles at Lizzie and ruffles her frizzy hair. Joan watches and feels sick.

'Shall I show you all round the flat?' says Dad,

14

eagerly. 'What do you think of the curtains? Lizzie made them. And wait till you see the patchwork quilt she made for the bed. Maybe Lizzie could teach you how to do patchwork, Jackie?'

'I think patchwork's boring,' says Jackie.

'Me too,' says Joan. '*I'm* bored. I want to go home.'

'But I don't have to take you home till seven,' says Dad. 'That's when Mum's expecting you.'

'I want to go home *now*,' says Joan.

'Joan! Don't talk to me like that,' says Dad, crossly.

'OK. I won't talk at all,' says Joan, and she shuts up again.

She doesn't even say goodbye to Lizzie.

'You're a silly, spoilt, rude little girl and I'm ashamed of you,' says Dad, when they're back in the car. 'And you're not much better, Jackie. I was really looking forward to this afternoon. I've told Lizzie so much about my two girls. I wanted to be proud of you.'

He goes on and on. Jackie takes no notice and reads her love comic. Joan takes no notice either. She opens her new pack of Plasticine and makes little plugs for her ears. For the first time ever she's glad when Dad says goodbye.

She's starving by this time. She sits at the kitchen table with Mum and Jackie and they have a cup of tea together and eat bread and jam, discussing Dad and this new Lizzie person. Joan eats *ten* slices of bread and jam and for once Mum doesn't try to stop her.

When Joan goes to bed, she takes the shoebox flat and looks at it mournfully. She takes out the round red Plasticine Joan and perches her up on the window sill. Then she squashes the beds, the table and chairs, the sofa, the bath, the lavatory. She squashes each and every gadget. Then she picks up Dad and squashes him flat.

Two

Joan pours herself a small bowl of cornflakes and doesn't even try to sneak more than the one permitted spoonful of sugar.

'What's wrong, Joan?' asks Mum, raising her eyebrows.

'What's *right?*' Joan replies.

'Now, I know you're upset about Dad—but it's maybe silly to take it too much to heart. I'm not sure this Lizzie will last long. She'll soon get fed up once she gets to know your Dad properly,' Mum says, cattily.

'I don't care about Dad and his stupid girlfriend anyway,' Joan lies, stirring her cornflakes, gloomily.

'Then why are you looking so down in the dumps, mm?'

'Because it's Monday morning and I've got five whole days of school and you know perfectly well I can't stick this horrible new school.'

'Oh, Joan. Don't start.'

But Joan has started. 'It's not *fair*. Jackie got to stay at her old school. *Why* did I have to swop?'

It's been pointed out a hundred times that Jackie's comprehensive is only three miles away, and she can get there on the bus without too much difficulty. Joan's old Junior school is now more than five miles away from their new flat, and not even on a proper bus route.

'This is supposed to be a much better school anyway,' says Mum. 'We were lucky to get you in. There's a waiting list, you know.'

'You'd have to be mad to want to go to Fairacre. It's so old-fashioned. The teachers are all morons. Or they're revoltingly strict. And the other kids are horrible.'

'You'll settle down soon, lovie, you'll see. You'll start to make friends and–'

'Catch me making friends with any of that lot!' says Joan. 'I hate them all. I hate this new flat. I hate this whole new life.'

'It's not much of a picnic for me either,' says Mum. 'I liked the old house much more, you know I did. But when Dad and I split up, we couldn't afford to keep it on. I liked my old job at the shop. I get all worried about this new office job. Working's much worse than school, you know. And my boss is going to do his nut when I ask for time off because the plumber's coming.'

Joan concentrates on her cornflakes. She wanted a bit of sympathy, not a boring old lecture. And Mum's wrong anyway. She's pretty sure Mum's boss doesn't threaten to stick Sellotape across her mouth because she's a chatterbox. And Mum's colleagues don't call her Fatty and whisper about her behind her back.

Joan walks to school, still sunk in gloom. Lots of children pass her but no-one talks to her, not even

18

to say hello. It's awful being so left out and unpopular. It's come as such a shock. At her old school she was always one of the favourites. No-one seemed to notice she was fat. Maybe it was because they all started in Class One of the Primary and grew up together. They all liked Joan because she was funny and had good ideas and could think up great games. Lots of people wanted to play with her at playtimes and sit next to her during lessons. The teachers liked her too. They laughed at her jokes and gave her stories and pictures big red ticks and picked her to read aloud or make a little speech to a visitor. When they did a Nativity Play Joan got to be Mary.

But it's all different at Fairacre. The class teacher is Miss Morpeth. And she's horrible. She's old, for a start, and very strict. Even the big boys don't mess about much with Miss Morpeth. No-one is allowed to play around at all. You have to sit up straight and listen to Miss Morpeth. When you know the answer to a question you have to put up your hand and wait to be asked. Joan isn't used to waiting. She's used to saying the first thing that comes into her head. She's also used to chatting happily as she does her work. Miss Morpeth says you mustn't talk at all, not even to your next door neighbour. Joan doesn't think much of Melvyn, the boy she sits next to in the classroom. He's very small and skinny and his face is usually screwed up into a frown. The other children tease him and call him Smelly Melly, so it's no wonder he looks worried. Joan doesn't think he'll make much of a

19

friend but she whispers witty little comments to try to cheer him up. It doesn't really work. Melvyn looks more anxious than ever and Miss Morpeth's bat ears twitch. Joan got told off for talking twelve times last Friday and Miss Morpeth threatened her with the Sellotape.

Joan glares now as she goes in the school gate. She's got Miss Morpeth teaching her all morning. She imagines getting a giant roll of Sellotape and winding it right round Miss Morpeth, wrapping her up like a parcel.

Joan goes into her classroom. Janice and Anita are standing between the desks. Anita is showing off some new shoes.

'Scuse me,' Joan mutters.

They take no notice, so she barges past them.

'Charming! Right on my foot. Like being trampled on by an elephant. If Fatty's scratched my new shoes I won't half sort her out.'

'You and whose army?' says Joan, fiercely. At first, she had hoped to make friends with Janice and Anita, but they've been hateful to her. Joan has to be hateful back, just to stay even.

Melvyn moves up nervously as she flounces into her seat. He scrabbles in his satchel for his books and pencils.

'Smelly Melly's looking in his handbag,' says Billy, and all the boys snigger.

'Lost your lipstick, Smelly Melly?' says Mike.

'I'll find it for you, shall I?' says Billy, and he snatches the satchel out of Melvyn's hands.

Melvyn stares at him, blinking rapidly.

'Give it back, please,' he says.

They imitate his voice, making him sound silly.
Melvyn blinks harder.

'Whatever you do, don't cry,' Joan mutters. 'Just
snatch it back.'

'I'm going to ignore them. They'll soon get fed
up,' says Melvyn.

They don't get fed up. They start throwing
Melvyn's satchel all round the classroom. Pens and
pencils fall out of it.

'Get it *back*,' Joan hisses. 'Here. *I'll* get it.'

She stands up and tries to grab the satchel from
Billy.

'Oh, Fatty wants to play Piggy in the Middle,'
says Billy, and he throws the satchel to Mike.

Mike is smaller than Billy, and Joan feels they are
more evenly matched. She hurls herself at Mike,
chopping her arms wildly in the air. He shrieks and
throws the satchel up in the air. It whirls over and
over—and lands at the feet of Miss Morpeth, who
has just come into the classroom.

'Children! Calm down at once. This room's like
a bear-garden. Joan Morgan! I might have known.
Would you mind telling me why you're attacking
Michael Robinson?'

'I'm not attacking, Miss Morpeth, I'm defend-
ing,' says Joan.

'Yes, well, it still looks like fighting to me.
You're going to find yourself in serious trouble if
you don't watch out.'

'And serious trouble with my mum, too,' Anita
hisses. 'These are Ravel shoes, you know, and

21

you've gone and made a big mark on them.'

Joan feels like making a great big mark all over Anita. She goes back to her desk, glowering. It's not *fair*.

She finds her own eyes are stinging. Melvyn gathers up his satchel and all his bits and pieces. He sits down next to Joan. She's still glowering, but he gives her a very timid smile. Joan perks up just a little.

Miss Morpeth takes the register and then starts talking about the Pied Piper of Hamelin. Joan vaguely knows the story: The Pied Piper was called to this town, Hamelin, hundreds of years ago, to rid it of a plague of rats. He charmed all the rats away with his magic flute but the Mayor and the Corporation quibbled over his payment so the Pied Piper came back and charmed their children away in revenge.

Miss Morpeth asks if anyone has heard the story before, but Joan doesn't put up her hand. She's decided she's not going to bother joining in any more. She's just going to sit in this classroom and think her own thoughts.

She doesn't listen properly when Miss Morpeth starts reading out the long poem about the Pied Piper. Miss Morpeth reads with a lot of expression, getting quite carried away, almost acting it out. Some of the childen laugh at the funny bits. They're all sitting up and paying attention. Joan slumps in her seat and yawns as often as she dares.

Almost at the end of the poem, when Miss Morpeth's voice is hushed as she describes the little lame boy who couldn't keep up with his playmates, Cathy comes rushing into the classroom.

'Sorry, I'm late, Miss Morpeth. Mum overslept and—'

'Sh! Go to your seat, Catherine. And come and see me after the lesson. You were late twice last week. It really isn't good enough.'

Cathy slinks miserably to the back of the class. Joan stares at her. It's not Cathy's fault she's late. It's her mum's, and Miss Morpeth knows it.

Joan glares at Miss Morpeth. If only a real Pied Piper would come bursting into the classroom in his strange red and yellow suit, with a magic pipe. Joan would be up and after him at the first note. Never mind the other children. Well, maybe Melvyn could come too. And Cathy? Just a few, specially chosen by Joan. And they'd dance after the Piper and he'd take them to the joyous land in the poem, where there are sparrows brighter than peacocks and horses with eagles' wings. Joan broods on them peacefully, deciding to have a go at modelling them in Plasticine.

Miss Morpeth has finished the poem and is talking away. Joan has long since stopped bothering to pay her any attention. And then she's suddenly aware of a silence. Miss Morpeth is looking at her.

'Well, Joan?' she says.

Joan stares at her, wondering what on earth she's been asked.

'What do you think of that idea?'

What idea? Oh help. Melvyn is trying to mouth

23

something at her but she can't work out what he's saying.

Joan shrugs and wrinkles her nose rather rudely.

'You don't seem very enthusiastic,' says Miss Morpeth. 'It's a pity. I'd have thought acting would be right up your street. Still, never mind. I'm sure there are plenty of others who want to be in the play.'

'What play?' Joan whispers to Melvyn.

'Her play. She's making a play out of the Pied Piper poem,' Melvyn whispers back.

'*Is* she?' Joan sits up properly. She can't pretend to be bored now. A play! Joan loves acting.

'Now, who's going to be the Pied Piper?' says Miss Morpeth.

'Me, Miss!' says Joan, jumping to her feet.

'I thought you didn't want to be in the play?' says Miss Morpeth.

'Oh, I've changed my mind,' says Joan, fervently. 'I'm ever so good at acting. I always had the lead part in the plays at my other school.'

She realizes she's boasting but she's got to let Miss Morpeth know.

'Then maybe it's time to give someone else a chance,' says Miss Morpeth. 'Besides, we want somebody very tall to play the Pied Piper—*and* someone who can play the recorder.'

There's a lot of discussion before Rory is chosen.

'Now, the Mayor,' says Miss Morpeth. 'I wonder who'd be right to play the Mayor?'

'He's "wondrous fat", it says so in the poem.' Janice giggles. 'You'd better pick Joan to be the Mayor, Miss Morpeth.'

There's a lot of laughter. Joan feels her face getting very hot. But she wouldn't mind playing the Mayor, even if he is fat. She knows she could act him in such a funny way that the children would laugh with her, not at her.

'OK, I'll be the Mayor,' says Joan, but Miss Morpeth picks Billy instead.

'What about us girls?' Joan complains.

Miss Morpeth chooses some girls to be members of the Mayor's Corporation. She still doesn't choose Joan. Then she casts the citizens of Hamelin. And then the children. Joan starts to get really worried. There are hardly any parts left.

'It's not fair,' she mutters to Melvyn. 'She's leaving me out on purpose.'

'I'm left out too,' says Melvyn.

'Yeah. We're the left-outs,' says Joan. 'It sounds good, that. Like a secret club.'

'We could be in a club, couldn't we?' says Melvyn.

'If you like,' says Joan, casually.

'Yes, I would like,' says Melvyn.

'Melvyn! It's not like you to be whispering,' says Miss Morpeth. 'Now, pay attention. There's still the part of the little crippled boy. A very important part.'

Joan fidgets in her seat, wondering whether to get up and manufacture an amazing limp to impress Miss Morpeth. But Miss Morpeth has already offered the part. To Melvyn.

Joan sighs.

'So I'm going to be left out all by myself,' she mutters.

'No,' says Melvyn. 'No, thank you, Miss Morpeth. I don't want to be the crippled boy.'

'Oh!' says Miss Morpeth. 'Very well, then. What about you, Michael? Do you want to be the little crippled boy?'

'Yes, I *feel* like a crippled boy after fighting with Joan,' says Mike.

Joan is staring at Melvyn.

'Why did you say no?' she asks.

'Well. So we could be left-outs together,' says Melvyn.

Joan is astonished. She knows she'd have jumped at the chance of being the crippled boy. She gives Melvyn a big grin.

'OK, pal. We're the Left-Outs,' she says.

'No-one is going to be left out of the play,' says Miss Morpeth, overhearing. 'Now, hands up all those children who haven't already got parts.'

Nine children put up their hands, including Joan and Melvyn.

'There's no need to look down-hearted,' says Miss Morpeth, brightly. 'You're all going to be in *The Pied Piper*. You're going to play very important parts. You're going to be the rats!'

Three

Joan feels insulted. She doesn't want to play a rat. Rats are her least favourite animals, for a start. She loves rabbits and guinea pigs. She's fond of hamsters. She can tolerate mice. She's not so sure about gerbils. But she knows one thing. She hates rats.

'We don't want to be rats, do we, Melvyn?' says Joan. 'We're going to be the Left-Outs. Let's tell Miss Morpeth.'

'I don't think that's a very good idea,' advises Melvyn.

Joan seldom listens to advice. She goes up to Miss Morpeth, who is busy discussing recorder tunes with Rory.

'Not now, Joan.'

'But Miss Morpeth—'

'Joan! Go and join up with the other rats, get in a little discussion group, take a copy of the poem from my desk, and read the rat verses together.

'Miss Morpeth, I don't want to be a rat.'

Miss Morpeth turns from Rory, and gives her full attention to Joan.

'I'm afraid you *are* a rat, Joan. If you hadn't been so silly at the beginning of the lesson I might well have picked you for one of major parts. But as it is,

27

you are a rat. And you'll just have to make the best of it.'

'I don't want to be a rat. I don't want to be in the play at all, thank you,' says Joan.

Miss Morpeth takes a deep breath. The children stare with interest. It looks as if Miss Morpeth is going to lose her temper.

'Joan Morgan. I have had just about enough of you for one morning,' she says. 'First you show no interest in the play whatsoever. Then you demand a starring part. And now you say you don't want to be in the play at all. Listen to me, Joan. I don't particularly want to have you in my classroom. But I'm afraid we're stuck with each other. And while you are in my classroom, you will also be in our play. As a rat. Do I make myself clear?'

'As crystal,' mutters Joan, and stumps back to her seat. 'It looks as if we're in her lousy play after all,' she says to Melvyn.

'Never mind. Couldn't we still be Left-Outs?' Melvyn suggests.

'But we're not left out, are we?' says Joan.

'Well. We are in a way. We're left out by most of the others. They don't want us in their games or anything.'

'I don't *want* to be in their boring, babyish games,' says Joan, pretending it's true. But then she smiles at Melvyn. 'OK. We'll still be Left-Outs. It's our own secret exclusive club, right? We can have a badge. And a password. And all sorts of weird rituals.'

'Not too weird, I hope,' says Melvyn.

'And we'll have to have a club leader, in charge of everything,' says Joan. 'I'll be it.'

'I thought you would be,' says Melvyn, but he doesn't seem to mind.

Miss Morpeth is looking in their direction.

'Will you join up with the other rats at once!' she shouts.

'What a way to talk to us!' Joan mutters. 'Still, I suppose we'd better do as she says.'

The other rats are sitting in a little bunch, not saying very much. There's Cathy, with her hair all tousled and traces of yesterday's baked beans down her grubby T shirt. There's Ryan, who's so strange and shy he never says a word to anyone. He always keeps his anorak on, as if he's kidding himself he can run home any minute. Sometimes he even pulls the hood up over his head. There's Louise and Pete, who always go round together. Joan thought they were brother and sister at first, because they've both got wispy, sandy hair and pale, pointy faces, but it turns out they just live at the same Bed and Breakfast Hotel. Then there's Tich, who's even smaller than Melvyn, but nowhere near as timid. He's got short skinhead hair and he inks pretend tattoos up and down his arms. There's Dawn, a big lumbering girl who wears fancy frocks that are too small for her. She looks like a big baby, and she's not very quick at learning so she sometimes acts like one too. And finally there's Summer, who's got long, flowing hair, a rose velvet waistcoat and an embroidered skirt that hangs right down to her ankles.

29

'Do any of you lot want to be rats?' Joan asks. They mostly shrug and shake their heads.

'Yes, it's daft, isn't it,' says Joan. 'Tell you what! How about if we all go on strike?'

'Yeah,' says Tich enthusiastically.

'We'll just sit here. We won't bother to read the rat bits in that boring old poem.'

'We'll get into trouble,' says Cathy.

'So what?' says Joan.

'So, she's got it in for me already, just because I was late,' says Cathy. 'We overslept. My mum was out late last night so me and my brothers and sisters, we watched this great horror video, all about this gigantic werewolf with a double set of teeth.'

'Tell us about it, then,' says Joan, reluctantly impressed. She doesn't even have a video at home any more. And when they did have one, before Mum and Dad split up, Mum never let her watch anything more stimulating than Mary Prissy Poppins.

So Cathy tells them all about the gigantic werewolf and its famous teeth. She tells them in exact detail how it bites and what it rips. Joan and Melvyn and Ryan and Louise and Pete and Tich and Dawn and Summer listen, enthralled. Joan bares her teeth and starts acting out a gigantic werewolf attack.

'Joan Morgan! What *are* you doing?' Miss Morpeth calls.

'I'm practising being a rat, Miss Morpeth,' Joan calls back.

'I've seen a video about killer rats, too,' says Cathy.

'Tell us about it,' says Tich.

'Yes, go on, Cathy.'

'Oh, that killer rat thing? I thought that was a bit tame,' Joan lies, badly wanting to impress. 'I've seen heaps worse than that.'

'Like what?' asks Cathy.

Joan thinks hard. She puts her hand in her skirt pocket and finds a little blob of left-over Plasticine. She fiddles with it for inspiration.

'Killer worms,' she says.

They snort with laughter.

'No, you just listen. This scientist invents a new fertilizer for everyone's garden, right, to grow these huge great flowers. Only it goes a bit wrong. The flowers stay the same. It's the worms that start growing. And the fertilizer enriches their brain cells so they start to get all sly and sneaky too. They start slithering about, just under the surface of the earth, so that they're still not spotted. You just see this wet pink coil glistening through the flower beds every now and then. And then they decide to take over. They writhe right under the back doors of all the houses. Some of the slimmer, slinky ones go up the drainpipes. Some even get into the sewer pipes and swim along and then come slithering up the lavatory—'

'Ugh! Shut *up*, Joan!'

'Imagine it, there's this girl very like you, Cathy, and you see her sitting on the loo and then—' Joan takes the wiggly piece of pink Plasticine and

31

suddenly flips it in Cathy's face.

Cathy squeals.

'What are you doing over in that corner?' Miss Morpeth thunders. 'If that's you being silly *again*, Joan . . .? What's that pink thing?'

Joan retrieves her Plasticine calmly. 'Oh, I was just thinking about costumes, Miss Morpeth. Wondering if you could make a good rat's tail out of Plasticine.'

'Are we going to have costumes, Miss Morpeth?' Cathy asks. 'Will our mums have to make them?'

'I hope we'll all lend a hand,' says Miss Morpeth. '*The Pied Piper* is going to be a proper play. Certainly we'll have costumes. We'll have a proper performance on the hall stage, with scenery.'

'In front of all the other forms, Miss Morpeth?'

'In front of your parents too. I want our form to show everyone just what's possible. I'm counting on you all.'

'I'm not so sure she should count on us lot,' Joan mutters. 'Hey, imagine if we all went on strike right in the middle of the play. There's old Rory as the Pied Piper trilling away on his recorder. And there's us rats lolling about on the stage, not the slightest bit interested in following him. And Miss Morpeth going purple with embarrassment at the side of the stage.'

'I think we'd better watch out. She'd go berserk if we did that. We'd better be in the play and do what she says,' Melvyn says, sensibly. He puts his head close to Joan's. 'And we'll still be Left-Outs. With you as the leader.'

He's not very good at whispering. 'What's a Left-Out?' says Cathy.

Joan hesitates, not sure whether to let the others in on the secret or not.

'Left-Out,' says Dawn. She thinks about it. 'I'm left out.'

'What are you on about, Daftie Dawn?' asks Cathy. 'What is this Left-Out thing, then? Tell us.'

'She doesn't know,' says Melvyn.

'I do. I'm left out. You lot won't play with me,' says Dawn.

'That's because you're daft,' says Cathy.

'Don't call her names,' says Joan.

'She *is* daft.'

'No, she's not. She *does* know,' says Joan. 'OK, Dawn. You're a Left-Out too. With Melvyn and me.'

'You're just being stupid too, Fatty,' says Cathy. 'Making out you've got this secret. You're just pretending. Same as all them killer worms. You never saw a real video like that. You were making it up.'

'I did see the video,' Joan insists, unwisely.

'Then bring it to school. Show us.'

'I can't. It's an adult video, I wasn't supposed to see it. My mum took it back to the shop.'

'You're just a big liar, Fatty.'

'If you call me that one more time I'll smash your teeth in,' says Joan.

'Why can't Cathy be a Left-Out too?' Melvyn says, quickly. 'And Louise and Pete. And Tich. And Summer. And Ryan. We could all be Left-

Outs, couldn't we? And you could still be the leader,' Melvyn adds.

'OK,' says Joan, after some consideration. 'Only there are certain rules and regulations, I hope you all understand. Number one is that you've got to do what the leader says. And number two is that no-one is allowed to call anyone stupid names like Daftie or Smelly.'

'Or Fatty,' says Cathy, giggling.

'You'd better watch yourself, Cathy,' says Joan. 'Or you might find yourself being left out of the Left-Outs.'

'See if I care,' says Cathy. But she doesn't call Joan Fatty this time.

'I think the Left-Outs are a great idea,' says Summer, jingling the little bells on her necklace. 'It's like we're an alternative society. Only why do we have to have a leader?'

'And why does the leader have to be a girl?' says Tich.

'Because I got the idea first,' says Joan. 'And I talked it over with Melvyn, so he gets to be my second-in-command, OK?'

Melvyn smiles gratefully.

'Smelly Melly couldn't command a Care Bear,' Tich mutters.

'You shut your mouth, Tich!' says Joan sharply.

'Tich is a nickname,' says Cathy. 'You'd better call him by his real name—' she pauses and sniggers—'it's Elton!'

'You shut up, Cathy. I'm Tich.' He clenches his fists, belligerently.

34

'Do you lot want to be Left-Outs or not? If so, you'd better swear allegiance,' says Joan.

'You what?' says Cathy, spluttering.

'Allegiance, Cloth Ears,' says Joan. 'It's like loyalty. You've got to swear to be loyal to me and the other Left-Outs.'

'What do you have to do when you're loyal?' Dawn asks.

'You've got to stick up for me and the others. Act like we're all special friends. And not tell anyone else what we do and what we say,' Joan explains.

'Yes, I can do that,' says Dawn.

'Then shake on it,' says Joan, offering Dawn her hand.

Dawn shakes it very thoroughly indeed.

'And say "I swear allegiance to the Left-Outs," ' says Joan, rubbing her fingers.

Dawn tries to say it, and gets a fit of the giggles. Joan prompts her sternly and eventually she gets it said.

Then Melvyn, Cathy and Tich say it. Summer laughs at the solemnity but says it too. Louise and Pete swear allegiance in unison.

'Fine. Now it's just you, Ryan,' says Joan. 'Shake my hand and swear allegiance.'

Ryan hesitates. He holds out his hand. Joan shakes it. 'And do the swearing allegiance bit,' she says.

Ryan goes on shaking but says nothing.

Joan sighs.

'Say "I swear allegiance to the Left-Outs".'

'Joan, Ryan doesn't talk,' says Cathy.

'Why doesn't he?'

'Don't ask me. He just doesn't. Not even to Miss Morpeth. They've sent him to special doctors and that, but he still never says a word.'

'Well, of course he can't feel very chatty bundled up in that anorak. It's just like a strait-jacket. Here, Ryan.' Joan reaches over and unzips the anorak. 'There, that's better, isn't it?'

Ryan certainly looks more comfortable, but he still doesn't speak.

'Maybe he's deaf,' says Louise. 'My little brother's got something wrong with his ear and he can't hear properly.'

'Are you deaf, Ryan?' Joan asks. She holds one of her ears and waggles it to make her point plain.

Ryan shakes his head.

'There. He's not deaf.'

'Maybe he don't speak English,' says Tich.

Joan considers.

'*Do* you speak English, Ryan?' she says, very slowly and clearly.

Ryan gives a shrug.

'What does that mean?' asks Tich.

Joan thinks carefully.

'I wonder what Miss Morpeth looks like without her clothes on,' she says, suddenly.

All the children giggle. And Ryan grins, fleetingly.

'He understands English all right. He just won't speak it,' says Joan. 'Well, Ryan. If you won't swear allegiance, you can't be in the Left-Outs.'

Ryan hangs his head.

'That's a bit heavy, Joan,' says Summer. 'Maybe he's really shy or something.'

'Maybe he's got a stammer,' says Melvyn. 'I used to stammer a bit when I was little. People laughed at me.'

'If he's left out of the Left-Outs he'll be all on his todd,' says Tich.

'Well, it's not my fault,' says Joan, uncomfortably 'Come on, Ryan. Stop being so awkward. Just say it. OK, forget the allegiance part. Just shake and say "I swear".'

Ryan shakes again, willingly enough. But he doesn't say a word.

'Whisper it,' says Joan.

Still nothing.

'Mouth it,' says Joan, desperately.

Ryan looks at her. He looks at all the other Left-Outs.

'Like this,' Joan says, and she mouths the words 'I swear'.

Ryan swallows. He licks his lips anxiously. And then he opens them. He mouths two silent words: 'I swear.'

'Hurray!' says Joan, and she shakes Ryan's hand vigorously. 'Now you're a Left-Out too.'

Ryan grins, then picks up a pencil and a piece of scrap paper. He starts drawing.

'What's that you're doing?' asks Joan. 'Oh yeah. That's a head and there's the arms and . . . Ryan! You dirty thing.'

'It's a lady,' says Dawn.

'Is she a pin-up?' asks Tich. 'Cor, look at her!'

But this seems to be an older woman, though she is posing stark naked with one hand on her hip. Ryan starts drawing in the facial details. Two beady eyes, a long nose, a cross mouth . . .

'It's Miss Morpeth without her clothes on!' Joan exclaims, delightedly.

All nine Left-Outs dissolve into floods of laughter.

'Whatever is going on over there?' Miss Morpeth shouts, standing up to peer at the giggling group. Unfortunately she puts her hand on her hip as she does so, which makes them splutter helplessly.

'Will you stop this!' Miss Morpeth commands, stalking over to them.

Joan quickly snatches the incriminating piece of paper out of Ryan's hand and stuffs it up the sleeve of her cardigan.

'Well?' Miss Morpeth demands, looming over them. 'I want an explanation!'

The Left-Outs look at each other.

'We were just getting excited about being rats in your play, Miss Morpeth,' says Joan, trying to look innocent. 'It's going to be *such* fun.'

'Hmm,' says Miss Morpeth, but the bell goes for the end of the lesson and she decides to give Joan the benefit of the doubt.

The Left-Outs leave the classroom in a little bunch, still giggling feebly.

'I like being a Left-Out,' says Dawn, and she dances clumsily down the corridor, her short skirt flying. She rounds the corner and bumps into

Janice, who is trying on one of Anita's famous new shoes.

'Watch where you're going, Daftie,' says Janice, pushing her.

'You watch where you're going. And don't call her Daftie,' says Joan, sticking up for Dawn.

Dawn herself isn't particularly concerned. She's looking at Anita's shoes.

'I wish *I* had lovely grown up shoes like that,' she says, sighing. 'Can I try one on too, Anita?' She bends to undo her sandals.

'No fear! I don't want your giant smelly great feet ruining my new shoes,' says Anita, nastily.

'Yes, look at Daftie's great clodhoppers,' says Janice, snatching at Dawn's loosened sandal. 'Imagine wearing this, eh!'

'You leave her alone. And give her back her sandal,' Joan shouts, rushing up to Janice.

'You shut up, Fatty,' says Janice, throwing the sandal over Joan's head to Anita.

'My sandal!' Dawn wails, her toes curling inside her sock. She hops about pathetically.

'Don't worry, Dawn. I'll get it back,' says Joan.

'We'll get it back,' says Melvyn.

'Hark at Smelly Melly,' Janice laughs.

'We'll *all* get it back,' says Cathy.

Ryan nods emphatically, taking his anorak right off to show he means business.

'Yes, we'll get it back for you, Dawn,' says Louise. 'Won't we, Pete?'

'You bet we'll get it back,' says Pete, staunchly.

Janice and Anita are starting to look worried.

39

'I think they're sensing the hostile vibes,' says Summer.

'Yeah. We're going to bash you up if you don't give it back,' says Tich.

'Here's your silly old sandal,' says Janice, hurriedly, and she throws it into a corner.

'What a silly fuss about an old sandal,' says Anita, and she starts running down the corridor.

She's still not used to the sophisticated style of her new shoes and she trips and nearly falls over.

'Quick! Or they'll get us,' Janice hisses, trying to pull her up.

They stumble away down the corridor, leaving the Left-Outs to laugh.

Four

Joan rushes home from school, humming happily. Melvyn hurries along beside her, still looking worried.

'Are you sure your mother won't mind me coming to tea with you?' he asks again.

He's diligently phoned his own mother to ask her permission. She seems very fussed about the whole idea, so Joan takes over the phone and does her best to persuade her. Melvyn's mum fusses even more, but Melvyn eventually talks her round.

'Of course my mum won't mind. *She* never makes a fuss about things,' Joan says, rather unkindly.

'You're lucky,' says Melvyn. 'What about your dad?'

'Who cares about boring old fathers?' says Joan, quickly. 'Come on, Melvyn. We've got heaps to do, especially if you've got to be home by seven o'clock. We've got to make nine badges for the Left-Outs. And some jewellery too.'

'Jewellery? Won't that cost too much?'

'Modelled out of Plasticine. And then I could do a blob of Plasticine like a medieval seal at the bottom of each sheet of rules and regulations. We've still got to work on them. That'll be one of the best bits,' says Joan.

'Are you allowed to play with Plasticine?' says Melvyn, enviously.

'I don't play,' says Joan. 'I model.'

'Doesn't your mother moan about it getting trodden into the carpet?' asks Melvyn.

'I can do what I like,' says Joan, showing off. 'I've got my mum well under control. Here's where we live. This grotty block of flats. It isn't a patch on our old house.'

They go up the stairs and along the balcony. Joan opens the door with her latchkey.

'Is that you, Joan?' Mum calls. 'Come here at once!' She sounds very cross indeed.

Joans finds her in the kitchen.

'Why aren't you at work, Mum?' she asks.

'I've had to stay off all day, waiting for the wretched plumber,' Mum hisses. 'My boss is naturally furious and feels he can't rely on me. I wouldn't be at all surprised if he gives me the sack. And then what are we going to do?'

'Well. There's no need to get cross with me. Mum, I've brought a–'

'There's every reason to get cross with you, Joan. Because when the plumber eventually turned up, he explained what was wrong. Someone has taken the lid off the cistern and tampered with the works inside. Deliberately snapped it in two.'

Joan swallows.

'Joan! How *could* you!'

'How do you know it was me?' Joan says. 'It could have been Jackie. Or—or you could even have done it, Mum. You could have walked in

42

your sleep last night, you know you haven't been sleeping that well, and you could have taken the cistern lid off, thinking in your dream it was your heavy casserole, say, and—'

'Joan! Will you stop this nonsense! You know perfectly well it was you. I just don't understand how you could be so naughty. I know you were upset about Dad yesterday, but that's no reason to set about systematically wrecking my lavatory!'

'I didn't mean to. I was just seeing how it worked and—and it sort of broke of.'

'And you didn't tell me!'

'Well. I would probably have got round to it eventually.' Joan realizes there's something else she's not got round to. 'Mum, what have we got for tea?'

'Never mind tea. You're not having any tea. Do you know how much that plumber charged me? You're going to have to pay me your pocket money until you're an old woman, do you hear me?'

'Yes, Mum. Listen. Can my friend have tea, even if I'm being punished?'

'What friend?'

'This friend,' says Joan, fetching poor Melvyn, who is lurking uncomfortably in the hall.

Mum looks horribly embarrassed. And surprised, too, when Melvyn shakes her by the hand and says how do you do. Joan's friends have never been male, meek and well-mannered in the past.

'How do you do,' says Mum, smiling in spite of herself. 'Is Joan really your friend?'

'Oh, yes,' says Melvyn.

'You've got a very funny taste in friends, that's all I can say, Melvyn,' says Mum. 'If Joan goes round to your house, my advice is, don't let her near the lavatory.'

'Mum!'

But at least Mum has stopped being so cross. She manages to rustle up a very good tea of frankfurter sausages, baked beans and tomatoes, with strawberry yogurt for pudding. She leaves them in peace to eat, too, so that Joan can pretend her frankfurter is a cigar and scrape round the baked bean sauce with her finger. Melvyn giggles at her, but his own manners remain impeccable.

He even stands up and shakes hands with Jackie when she trails home from school. Jackie chats to him in a friendly way but when she goes off to find Mum, Joan hears suspicious splutters.

'Idiots,' says Joan loftily.

'I think they're very nice,' says Melvyn.

'They're going to tease me rotten because they'll think you're my boyfriend,' says Joan. 'They don't have a clue we're the leader and second-in-command of a very exclusive and special secret society. Shall I help you finish that yogurt, Melvyn? Then we can get cracking on the badges and the jewellery and that.'

They spend a very happy hour in Joan's bedroom, tracing round a ten-pence piece onto cardboard and cutting out the circles. Joan writes the initials L.O. on each badge and Melvyn fixes a safety pin to each one.

'Now for the jewellery,' says Joan.

'I'm not sure that's really a good idea. Not for the boys,' says Melvyn.

'Don't be so sexist,' says Joan.

'Yes, but the boys all tease me like mad as it is. If I start wearing jewellery then they'll do their nuts.'.

'I'm not suggesting you boys deck yourself out in brooches and necklaces,' says Joan. 'Imagine Tich in a necklace! No. Rings. Discreet signet rings to be worn on the little finger. Brilliant!'

'What colour?'

'Yellow, so it looks like gold. And you'd better start collecting up some of the red, to make the seals for the list of rules and regulations. There's only two little strips in this new packet and I can't buy any more if Mum's going to commandeer my pocket money, the meanie old thing. So I'll just have to use up this old stuff,' says Joan, retrieving some of the squashed pieces from the shoebox.

There's still not enough yellow and red to go round, so Joan has to plunder the little yellow Plasticine people mountaineering up her bedroom curtains and tightrope-walking along her picture rails, and the little lost tribe of red Plasticine people camping in the fluff under her bed.

'All this yellow and red. It's like the Pied Piper's suit,' says Melvyn.

'Don't say anything about that to Mum and Jackie. They won't half laugh at me when they know I'm going to be a rat,' says Joan. 'The humiliation!'

'It might be quite good fun,' says Melvyn.

'You've got to be joking,' says Joan. She gives him a sideways look. 'Any regrets about not being the little crippled boy?'

'No. I'd much sooner be with my friends,' says Melvyn. 'Here. All the red seals are done now. What are we going to put for the rules? The one about obeying the leader?'

'Naturally,' says Joan. 'And the one about no nicknames. Although we can have a special dispensation in Tich's case, as he doesn't mind his.'

'And is that it?'

'Of course not! We've got to think of heaps.' Her eyes sparkle. 'We could have one rule where everyone has to bring the leader a special snack to eat at playtime. And we could have another where the leader gets an official Left-Outs birthday as well as her own real one, and everyone has to bring her an official birthday present.'

'Are you serious, Joan?' asks Melvyn.

'Not really,' says Joan, wistfully.

'We ought to do it properly,' says Melvyn.

'Don't you ever like mucking about?' says Joan. She sighs. 'OK. OK. Now, rule number three . . .'

'I'm not even sure about rule number one,' says Melvyn, a little timidly. 'The one about obeying the leader.'

'Is this a mutiny or something?' says Joan.

'No. Not at all. It's just that I think there ought to be a special dispensation thingy. I mean. Supposing you said, "Right, all Left-Outs have got to poke out their tongues at Miss Morpeth".'

'Well?' says Joan, grinning.

'Well, that would be stupid, wouldn't it, because we'd all get into trouble.'

'Not necessarily. We could all pick and choose our moments. We could poke out our tongues when her back's turned. Or do it whilst hiding behind a desk lid. Or—'

'Joan. That's not the point. Supposing you said, "All Left-Outs have got to jump out of the window".'

'I sometimes wish you'd jump out of the window, Melvyn.'

'But you do see my point, don't you, Joan? You could get us to do anything that way.'

'That's what being a leader is all about.'

'Well, suppose someone else got to be leader. How would you like it if you always had to do what I said? Or Cathy? Or Tich?'

Joan sighs, but has to concede that Melvyn has a point. She'd thought he was this silly timid little guy who'd do exactly what she wanted. He acts that way at school. But out of school he seems to be a different person altogether.

'OK, OK. Rule number one is that all Left-Outs have to obey their leader—but only when it seems sensible. Right?' says Joan, flicking a piece of Plasticine in Melvyn's face.

'Right,' says Melvyn, blinking. 'Joan! Stop it. We'll never get these rules written out.' He ducks the multi-coloured hailstorm as best he can. He looks at his watch. 'Oh gosh. I'd better get home anyway.'

'Oh Melvyn. You've only just got here. Stay for

47

a bit longer. Your mum won't mind,' says Joan.

'She will,' says Melvyn.

'Well, it's not fair. Have I got to write out all these poxy rules and regulations by myself?'

'I'll take them home with me and do it, if you like,' says Melvyn.

'Oh. Will you? Well, your writing's much neater than mine anyway,' says Joan. 'And I have done all these rings. What do you think of them?'

'They look great.'

'I'll emboss a couple to make them look really good,' says Joan, making a zigzag pattern with the tip of her pen.

'You're going to muck your pen up, doing that.'

'Yes, but it looks really artistic, doesn't it,' says Joan. 'Which do you like the best?'

'That one.'

'Oh. So do I.' Joan struggles. 'Still, never mind. You can have it, even though I'm the leader and ought really to get the best ring.'

'No, it's OK. I'll have the other one.'

'Melvyn. I said take it.' Joan puts it on his little finger. 'I feel like I'm asking you to marry me.'

'Melvyn blinks nervously.

'I'm *joking*, Melvyn.'

'Marrying you would certainly be a joke, Joan,' says Melvyn. 'Joan? Stop it! *I* was joking. Get off me! Help!'

Five

Joan gets to school early the next morning and presents each Left-Out with their badge and Plasticine ring. Melvyn hands out the lists of rules and regulations. He's made a beautiful job of them too, copying out the rules in his best italic handwriting, and working an individual design, with a pin, on each red Plasticine seal. Joan's seal has the word Leader and a crown and a glittery trail of stars—but she frowns when she looks at the rules.

Melvyn has added a new rule.

'All Left-Outs must stick up for each other.'

'What's this then? I never said anything about it,' Joan says, suspiciously.

'I thought of it, Joan. It seemed like a good idea. So I put it in,' says Melvyn.

Joan swallows. Melvyn isn't the Leader. She is.

'Don't you think it's a good rule?' says Melvyn.

'That's not the point,' says Joan. 'It's not actually your place to make up any rule, good or bad.'

Melvyn looks worried.

'Oh, cheer up. I suppose it was a good idea. Just consult with your leader first, before making any more major decisions,' says Joan.

The other children are interested in the distinctive badges and rings and sheets of rules.

'What does L.O. mean then? And why are you all wearing those funny rings? And what's that writing say?'

'Never you mind,' says Joan, with a maddening grin on her face.

The other Left-Outs mostly copy her example. Ryan is certainly not going to give any information away. But there's always Dawn, who's too friendly for her own good.

'What's this silly secret you lot have got with Joan Morgan, Dawn?' asks Janice.

'What does L.O. stand for, Dawn?'

Dawn giggles. 'Joan doesn't want me to tell.'

'I bet you don't even know. You're too stupid to know,' says Anita artfully.

'I do know!' says Dawn.

'L.O. It doesn't stand for anything.'

'It does!' says Dawn.

'Maybe they've just spelt it wrong. Maybe it should be L.O.O. Loo. The Toilet Club,' says Anita.

Janice shrieks with laughter. 'Yeah, that's your precious secret club, isn't it, Dawn? It's the Toilet Club. And you write out all your secret rules on a piece of toilet paper.'

'We don't! It's all written out on lovely paper, with a red blob thing called a seal,' says Dawn.

'Let's see then,' says Anita.

'All right,' says Dawn, and starts to fish her folded paper out of her pocket.

But Joan sees and comes flying across the classroom.

'Put that back!' she commands Dawn, dragging her away from Janice and Anita.

She gets Dawn in a corner.

'Now listen, Dawn,' she says. 'If you can't keep all this a secret you can't be in the Left-Outs, right? You mustn't show our special rules to anyone else.'

'But they said we had a silly toilet club. I wanted to show them we didn't, we've got a proper club.'

'They were just trying to trick you, Dawn. Don't you go round with Janice and Anita or any of the others. You stick with us Left-Outs, OK?'

At playtime Joan makes Melvyn add another rule to everyone's list:

'The Left-Outs must never divulge any of their secrets'.

'You've still not said what we're actually going to *do*,' says Cathy. 'We're this secret club, The Left-Outs, right. But what do we do?'

'We stick up for each other,' says Melvyn.

'I don't need anyone to stick up for me,' says Cathy. 'I can stick up for myself.'

'And we play with each other,' says Dawn.

'Maybe we could have adventures,' says Louise. 'Look for suspicious goings-on and that.'

'Have you been reading them Enid Blyton books?' says Cathy, sighing.

'The trouble with you, Cathy, is that you're always moaning,' says Joan.

Joan does her fair share of moaning in the afternoon, because Miss Morpeth devotes all three lessons to *The Pied Piper*. She hands around print-outs of the script.

'There's page after page of it!' says Billy. 'Have we really got to learn all these lines, Miss Morpeth?'

'Of course, Billy.'

'I don't reckon this Mayor lark. I don't think I'll be it after all.'

'You'll do as you're told,' says Miss Morpeth, crisply.

'It all sounds so funny,' says Janice, flipping through her print-out. 'I've got to say this long speech about the rats, and how they're a plague and an abomination and this other stuff. It sounds daft. People don't talk like that.'

'They did in Hamelin hundreds of years ago,' says Miss Morpeth, crossly.

'Hamelin's in Germany, isn't it, Miss Morpeth?' says Joan. 'So they spoke German. Maybe we could all click our heels and strut about and say *Ja* and *Nein*.'

Most of the children immediately start gabbling their lines in atrocious German accents. Miss Morpeth claps her hands furiously. '*The Pied Piper* is a serious play, not a comic show.'

'Maybe it would be better if it was a comedy, Miss Morpeth. It looks ever so boring,' Joan persists, unwisely.

'It's not at all boring,' snaps Miss Morpeth. She wrote the script herself and prides herself on her literary talents. 'If I have one more ridiculous comment from you, Joan Morgan, you are going to be in very serious trouble. Now, children, we might as well make a start. The first scene. That's the rats. All the rats come out to the front of the class.'

The Left-Outs trail forward self-consciously. Joan is consulting her print-out anxiously.

'Miss Morpeth, I think there's some mistake!'

'I thought I told you to be quiet, Joan.'

'Yes, but I think there's a page missing from my copy of the play. I haven't got a proper Scene One. My bit just says "Scene One. Rats!" And that's it.'

'Yes. That's it.'

'But where are our lines?'

'You don't have any lines, Joan. Neither do any of the other rats.'

'Lucky things!' says Billy.

But Joan doesn't think she's lucky at all.

'Don't we get to say anything?' she asks, devastated.

'When did you ever hear of a talking rat, Joan?' asks Miss Morpeth.

The children laugh. Joan looks upset.

'Don't argue with her. There's no point,' Melvyn hisses.

'But there are lots of plays where animals get to speak, Miss Morpeth,' Joan says. 'I went to see *Toad of Toad Hall* and there's a Rat in that and he gets to say heaps.' She nods her head to emphasize the point.

'You are not in *Toad of Toad Hall*. You are in *The Pied Piper*,' says Miss Morpeth. 'Although if you carry on with this behaviour I will not allow you to be in my play at all. Now *be quiet!*'

Even Joan sees that it's time to shut up.

'Now. Scene One. Rats,' says Miss Morpeth. 'The curtains will open. You will come on stage. You will act out a little piece, showing that you're the most terrible pest of Hamelin town.' She glances at Joan. 'Some of you will find this task easier than others.'

Joan glowers.

'I'll read out the rat verse to give you all a little inspiration,' says Miss Morpeth. She finds her place in her poetry book, and begins:

' "They fought the dogs and killed the cats,
    And bit the babies in the cradles,
    And ate the cheeses out of the vats,
    And licked the soup from the cooks' own ladles,
    Split open the kegs of salted sprats,
    Made nests inside men's Sunday hats,
    And even spoiled the women's chats,
    By drowning their speaking
    With shrieking and squeaking
    In fifty different sharps and flats." '

'Squeak. S-q-u-e-a-k. S-Q-U-E-A-K!' goes Joan.

'Joan!'

'I'm just getting inspired, Miss Morpeth.'

'Yes. Well. Good for you. But perhaps you could squeak a little more quietly while we're all crammed into the classroom at close proximity. Now, off you go, rats. Act out the verse. But *quietly*, Joan. This is just a rehearsal.'

It is not a success. Ryan doesn't join in at all. He stands in a corner, hanging his head. Louise and

54

Pete sit down and mime the consuming of cheese and soup, eating in a very un-ratlike way with pretend knives and forks and spoons. Dawn ambles across the floor on her hands and knees, going 'Squeak, squeak, squeak' in a monotonous manner. Melvyn curls up under Miss Morpeth's desk, doing an elaborate mime of nest-making inside a man's Sunday hat, but unfortunately none of this is at all visible. Joan and Tich and Cathy fight imaginary dogs with their fists. They kill imaginary cats with guns. They bite imaginary babies so savagely they all but sever them in two. And Summer sits cross-legged in their midst, being a sit-down pacifist rat, murmuring 'Cool it, fellow rats.'

'Will you stop this fiasco!' Miss Morpeth shouts. 'Really! Are you all being silly on purpose? For goodness sake, when have you ever seen a rat having a fist fight?'

'I've never seen a wild rat,' says Joan. 'I've seen a pet one in a cage, and it was on its own so it couldn't have a fight even if it tried. It looked disgusting, actually.'

'There are rats in our hotel,' says Louise.

'Yeah, we saw one in the kitchen once. My mum complained to the council, because it's horrible having to live in a place with rats,' says Pete.

'The rats are only looking for shelter, same as you,' says Summer. 'We tamed a rat in this squat where I used to live. Jet used to walk around with it perched on her shoulder.'

'Yes, well, stop chattering, children,' says Miss Morpeth. 'I'm going to have a serious think about this rat sequence. I don't want it to develop into a silly pantomime. Now, sit down for the moment, rats, and we'll go on to Scene Two, with the Mayor and his Corporation.'

Miss Morpeth spends the next few days going over the play. Joan and the other Left-Outs get very bored while the rest of the class stumble and stutter through their lines.

'When's it going to be the rats' turn again, Miss Morpeth?' Joan enquires.

Janice and Anita are playing two Hamelin women and Joan has worked out a little routine for herself in which she'll jump right up at them, snapping her rodent teeth and issuing piercing ratty shrieks and squeaks.

But Miss Morpeth has other plans.

'I've fixed up for you to be coached by Miss Banks,' says Miss Morpeth.

'Miss Banks?' says Joan, who hasn't got all the teachers properly sorted out yet.

'She's one of the Infants' teachers. She does Music and Movement,' says Melvyn.

'Not that stuff when you have to scrunch up and be little weeny bunny rabbits and then lumber around waving your trunks, being elephants?' says Joan, appalled. 'Oh no!'

Oh yes. They're sent along to find Miss Banks in the Infants' Hall. She's a toothy woman in a lavender tracksuit. She doesn't seem to notice that the nine Left-Outs are large Juniors. She treats them all as though they were Form One Infants.

'Now, children. Spread out nicely. Close your

eyes. No peeping now! That's it. Oh goodness! You're not children at all. You're rats. Big rats. Little rats. Fat rats.'

Joan snorts indignantly.

'Old rats. Young rats. There you are, quivering your noses, twitching your whiskers. And in a moment, when I play your special rat music, I want you to start moving across the hall. First the music will be very slow, so you'll move very slowly too. Then it will get faster and you'll start to skip and scurry. And then it will get faster still and, my goodness, you'll streak past me so fast I'll scarcely see you. Ready? Now!'

She starts playing the piano. The Left-Outs stand and stare at her.

'Come on!' she commands. 'Get moving, rats.'

They lumber into action.

'No, no! Try to feel like a rat!' calls Miss Banks.

'I don't feel like a rat, I feel like a prat,' Joan says to Melvyn.

'No talking, Fat Rat! And get moving, Skinny Rat.'

'Fat Rat's going to bash her goofy teeth in if she calls me that again,' Joan mutters.

The piano music quickens and they start to scurry. Dawn still has her eyes tightly shut, as originally commanded, and bumps into everyone.

'Watch what you're doing, Clumsy Rat! Dear, oh dear, you're not entering into the spirit of things at all.'

'Well, it's daft, Miss,' says Tich. 'I hate this sort of soppy dancing. Real rats don't prance about.'

'These are stage rats. Stage rats can dance,' says Miss Banks.

But when the music gets faster still and Summer decides to leap and whirl and kick up her legs in an elegant and athletic way, Miss Banks still isn't satisfied.

'No, no, Long-haired Rat. You're not a bird or a fairy or a leaf in the wind. They do that sort of dance. You're a *rat*.'

The Left-Outs are painfully reminded every day that they are rats. *The Pied Piper* seems to have taken over altogether. And there's going to be a grand performance in front of the parents at the end of term.

'But it's weeks and weeks and *weeks* before the end of term, so why do we have to keep fussing about it all now,' Joan moans in the Art lesson. 'It's not fair.'

Joan has always enjoyed Art. Even Miss Morpeth says her paintings are good and pins them on the wall. But today in Art, Joan's not allowed to do a proper picture. She's been put in charge of making nine rat masks. Melvyn cuts them out of cardboard and attaches elastic at the sides. Joan paints on the features. She quite enjoyed making the first mask. And the second. But now she's on the sixth or seventh and she's thoroughly fed up with the whole idea.

'Stupid, boring, silly play,' she mutters, splashing black paint all over the place.

'Careful!' says Melvyn, rubbing at his shirt sleeve anxiously.

'I'm sick of stupid, boring, silly rats,' says Joan, and she paints two red slitty eyes and huge yellow teeth on the rat mask.

'Ugh! Joan, that rat looks really evil,' says Melvyn, shuddering.

'Yes, he does, doesn't he?' says Joan, cheering up a little. 'I think I'm going to bag this mask.'

She gets a finer brush and fiddles around, sharpening the expression, making the rat leer in a terrifying way.

'He doesn't really look very ratty now,' says Joan, thoughtfully. 'More like a little demon.'

She paints two very tiny pointed horns on top of his head, and laughs.

'Look, Melvyn.' She holds the mask in front of her face and leers at him.

'Joan! Stop it! It looks *awful*,' says Melvyn, cowering away from her.

'I'm putting the Evil Eye on you, Melvyn,' says Joan, in a cackling, demonic voice.

'Take it *off*!'

'I wish we could do a play about a whole load of Demons doing black magic,' says Joan, staring at the mask. 'This could be the Leader Demon, the worst of the lot. The one that gets all the really wicked ideas and works the blackest magic. And there are all these other Demons too—and they wreak a magical, devilish revenge on all their enemies.'

'It sounds fun,' says Melvyn, wistfully.

'Heaps more fun than the Pied Piper and all these rotten old rats,' says Joan, starting a new mask.

'This can be the Demon who's second-in-command. The Leader's best friend.' She slaps on paint hastily. Melvyn's shirt gets spattered again but this time he doesn't even notice.

'Can he have really savage, pointy teeth? And little horns?'

'You bet,' says Joan.

'And is it my mask, Joan?'

'Of course it's your mask. Do you know what, Melvyn? We're going to do our own play. About Demons and evil and black magic and wicked revenge. A play just for us Left-Outs. We'll show that stupid Cathy. *That's* what the Left-Outs are going to do!'

Six

'How's this famous play getting on?' Mum asks, when she gets home from work.

'Depends which one you mean,' says Joan, smiling mysteriously.

'*The Pied Piper*,' says Mum, starting to unpack her shopping bags. 'Come on, Joan, Jackie, give us a hand.'

'You sit down, Mum. I'll do it,' says Jackie.

'And I'll make you a nice cup of tea, eh?' says Joan.

'Gosh. I think I've come back to the wrong home by mistake,' says Mum. 'Where are the two grumpy, grouchy girls who usually live here?'

'Oh, we must have our jolly little joke, mustn't we, Mummy-Chummy,' says Joan, putting on the kettle.

'No boyfriend tonight, Joan?' Mum asks, grinning.

'He walked her home from school,' says Jackie. 'Carying all her bags for her. Quite the little gent.'

'You shut up. He was helping me carry some props for our play,' says Joan, loftily. 'And at least Melvyn's got exquisite manners. Not like that oaf Mick. Honestly Mum, he phoned up just now, and I happened to answer it, and when he said it was him I did my best to be friendly, telling him it was a pity he'd missed the disco the other week, and he was so rude. He just said "Can I speak to Jackie?" He didn't even say please.'

'Oh! So Mick rang, did he, Jackie?' says Mum, eyebrows raised.

'Mmm,' says Jackie, her face very pink. 'I'm probably seeing him Saturday night.'

'Oh, yes?' says Mum.

'And actually, there's a whole crowd going up to the Heath on Sunday. There's some sort of fair on. Is it OK if I go to that, too?'

'But you're meant to be seeing your Dad, Jackie,' says Mum. 'You always see him on Sundays.'

'Well, exactly. So one Sunday won't make that much difference. And actually, I haven't really seen the point recently. It's OK for Joan, you know how she feels about Dad. And she *likes* trailing round zoos and parks. But I'm a bit old for that lark now. So I don't have to go, do I, Mum?'

'Well. I don't suppose so. You don't mind having Dad to yourself next Sunday, do you, Joan?' asks Mum.

Joan throws teabags into the pot, pressing her lips together fiercely. She won't have Dad to herself, that's the point. Dad's got Lizzie now.

'Joan! Steady on. We don't need six teabags!' says Mum.

'Sorry', says Joan, fishing them out. 'Actually Mum, I don't think I'll be able to see Dad either. I've got a lot of work to do on this play.'

'What? Joan, don't be silly. I didn't think you

even wanted to be in the play. I thought you were insulted because you've been picked to play a rat.'

'Well, who wouldn't be insulted?' says Joan, pouring in the hot water. 'No, I didn't mean that boring old Pied Piper piffle. I mean *my* play.'

'What play's this?'

'Oh, it's a secret play. I couldn't possibly tell you,' says Joan, maddeningly.

'Well, anyway, of course you must see Dad on Sunday,' says Mum, firmly. 'You can work on your play on Saturday.'

'Mum, I'm going to dedicate the entire weekend to my play,' says Joan, equally firmly. 'There are eight other people depending on me. And I don't want to see Dad. It's not fair. Jackie can get out of seeing him, so why can't I?' She gives Mum her cup of tea, banging it down rather hard, so that some spills into the saucer.

'Hey,' says Mum, catching hold of Joan before she can dart away. 'I know you're upset about this girlfriend of his. I'm not sure it was a good thing for Dad to introduce you at this stage—it probably won't last long anyway.' Mum gives a little sniff. 'But you know just how much Dad loves and cares about you, Joan. He misses you a lot. He'll be so hurt if you can't make it on Sunday.'

'So, he'll just have to be hurt,' says Joan. 'I'm sure William Shakespeare didn't have to take time off from writing his plays to go out with his dad.'

She sticks to her guns. Mum makes her phone Dad to tell him. Joan feels sick when she says it. She feels even worse when Dad sounds very upset.

63

But then she hears Lizzie in the background saying 'What is it, darling, what's the matter?' in her girly, gushing way. Joan feels sicker than ever and slams the phone down.

She spends a lot of Saturday and Sunday making little Plasticine models of Lizzie and stamping on them. She stamps one right into the carpet and can't scrape it all up again. She moves the rug over the Plasticine part hastily, and decides she'd better concentrate on her demon play instead.

She's promised the Left-Outs that she'll bring them their very own play on Monday morning. But writing plays isn't quite as easy as all that. She can make up all sorts of things and tell them to people without any bother at all. But when she comes to write it all down she very quickly runs out of things to put. Melvyn has given her a nearly new exercise book and lent her his special italic pen for inspiration.

Joan practises elaborate italic handwriting for half an hour. She ends up with an entire page of Joan Morgans—and still not one word of the play written.

After Sunday tea with Mum she gives up on the italic pen, seizes a pencil, and starts scribbling in sheer desperation. Mum is watching some people singing hymns on the television, not quite the right atmosphere when you're trying to write an outrageous, wicked and terrifying play about Demons, but Joan does her best.

She calls the main Demon Morgaslurp. She whispers her name to herself, pleased with it. She doesn't feel like wasting time naming all the other Demons, so she simply labels them Demon Two, Demon Three, etc. Morgaslurp is their all-powerful, inventive and totally evil leader. Most of the time she lives in a naturally centrally-heated cave in Hell, but occasionally she surfaces in the real world to wreak havoc. She gives a bossy, old-fashioned, elderly teacher a hairy wart on the end of her nose. She makes a big bully of a boy shrink down to six centimetres and locks him up in a cage with a hamster, who terrorizes him. She makes the feet of a show-off, spiteful girl grow until they're a man's size twelve and the only shoes she can find to fit are huge ugly lace-ups. She very nearly makes a fellow female Demon go cross-eyed after watching too many video films but magnanimously decides against this when the fellow Demon begs for mercy. But Morgaslurp shows no mercy whatsoever when she encounters a monster called Fatheramous who lives in a lair with a poisonous hairy spider called Dizzylizzie.

Joan writes page after page of terrible tortures, smiling grimly. She can't quite decide how to end her play. There could be one gloriously violent ending where Fatheramous and Dizzylizzie expire altogether. Or perhaps Morgaslurp tramples on Dizzylizzie and when the last drop of poison has been squeezed out of her, then her enchantment is broken and Fatheramous is free of her spell at last. So Morgaslurp takes pity on him and adopts him as a sort of pet, keeping him on a special collar and lead so that he's always under her control.

Yes. She likes that ending better.

'The End,' Joan writes at the bottom of her page, and then stretches her aching arms and sighs with satisfaction.

'I bet Shakespeare never wrote a whole play in one evening,' she says.

She can't wait to show it to the other Left-Outs. Melvyn calls for her so they can walk to school together. Joan insists on reading her play aloud to him on the way. She gabbles it quickly and Melvyn has to concentrate hard to follow the action, whilst steering Joan over the road and round the lampposts and parking meters.

Joan gets to the end just as they reach the school gate.

'How's that for timing?' she says. 'Well? What did you think of it, Melvyn? Isn't it good?'

'Yes,' says Melvyn, but he sounds a little doubtful.

'Imagine, I wrote it all just yesterday evening—look, there are pages and pages of it. Don't you think Morgaslurp is an incredible character?'

'Yes,' says Melvyn again. 'But—but she's really the only character.'

'What do you mean? There are all these people she torments.'

'So have all us Left-Outs got to play the people Morgaslurp torments?' asks Melvyn.

'No! Well, some of the time. But mostly you're the other Demons.'

'But they don't do anything.'

'Well. You can all improvise. Oh, Melvyn, it's

66

easy enough to criticize. *You* try writing a play.'

'I'm sorry, Joan. It's ever so good. Really.'

'Yes. I think it is too,' says Joan, still a little wounded.

She rounds up all the Left-Outs at lunchtime and gives another star performance of her play, gobbling down her cheese and pickle sandwiches, salt and vinegar crisps, mini Mars bar, apple and orange juice during the performance. She develops severe hiccups but even this doesn't deter her and she finishes her Morgaslurp saga triumphantly.

'Well?' she says. 'Don't I even get a clap?'

'I think it's ever so good,' says Dawn, loyally.

'I thought it was a bit boring,' says Cathy. 'The torture bits weren't really disgusting. I was watching this video last night and honestly, you just wait till I tell you what they did to this—'

'Shut *up*, Cathy. Never mind your stupid video. We're here to discuss our play. And it's not boring. Heaps and heaps of things happen.'

'Yes. But they all happen to you,' says Cathy. 'You'd be playing Morgaslurp, wouldn't you?'

'Well. Of course.'

'Couldn't we all take turns playing Morgaslurp?' Summer suggests.

'That would just get muddling,' says Joan.

'I don't want to be in a silly play anyway,' says Tich. 'It's bad enough having to do this Pied Piper lark. Miss Morpeth says we've got to wear tights. I'm not wearing flipping tights! What would all my mates say?'

'We're your mates now. And never mind *The*

Pied Piper. We're talking about our play. And of course you want to be in it. You could be Fatheramous if you like. That's a really big part. You ought to be big to play him, but I don't suppose it really matters.'

'I'll be the Spiderwoman,' says Summer, waving her fingers with spidery menace.

'She's not Spiderwoman, she's Dizzylizzie. But OK. And you're a Demon too, of course.'

'How can we be both? Often they're all going to be on stage together,' asks Melvyn.

'We'll work something out,' says Joan. That point's been bothering her too.

'Shall we get some of the others to be in the play too?' asks Dawn. 'Janice and Anita keep on asking me what we're up to. I think they'd like to be in it.'

'Well, they're not going to be. They're not Left-Outs.'

'My Demon's going to be called Winter,' says Summer. 'She's going to be really selfish, you know. She doesn't want to share. She just wants to dominate. And she's into violence in a big way. I'm going to make her live in this cave in Hell and she's going to make everyone do exactly what she says and if they won't, she'll take her pitchfork and—'

'No, she won't!' says Joan. 'That's not in my play at all.'

'Well, it is in mine,' says Summer, serenely.

'*My* Demon's going to be called Cathykiller and she's going to—'

'No, she's not!' says Joan, furiously.

'Joan,' says Melvyn. 'Why don't we have your

68

play as the main play, with you as Morgaslurp and us all acting your people that you torment. Then we could have another, linked play, with Summer's Demon and we could all play her people. And then one for Cathy. We could all have our own play about our own Demon.'

Joan thinks hard. She's not keen on this idea at all. But she's quick to see that this is probably the only way to keep all the Left-Outs interested.

'OK. Yes. We'll do that,' she says. 'Although I think you'll all find out just how jolly difficult it is to write a play for yourself. Still. If that's what you want . . . And I'll be the Director in Chief, OK?'

'Pete and me will do a play together. We can be twin Demons,' says Louise.

'My Demon's going to be huge. And he's going to go round bashing everyone up,' says Tich. 'He wouldn't wear tights in a million years. He'd just growl and rip them all to pieces.'

'My Demon's still going to be little. All weedy and wimpy. So people *think* they can bully him. But he's so immensely clever that he outwits them all, easy as anything,' says Melvyn.

There are two Left-Outs looking left out. One is Dawn. The other is Ryan.

'I don't know how to do a Demon,' says Dawn, worriedly.

'You've just got to write your own little play,' says Melvyn.

'I don't know how to write a play. I hate writing,' says Dawn.

'See, Melvyn,' says Joan. But then she goes to

Dawn and puts her arm round her. 'It's OK. I'll help you.'

'Will you really help me, Joan?'

'Yes, of course I will. What do you want your Demon to be called?'

'Dawn,' says Dawn.

'No, you've got to elaborate on your name.'

'I'm not being called Dafty Dawn.'

'Of course not. Look, we'll just call you Demon-Dawn, how about that? And you get to torment whoever you want. Who'd you like to torment, Dawn? Janice and Anita? They're always getting at you.'

'Yes, but I don't want to hurt them. I want them to be my friends,' says Dawn.

Joan sighs. 'You know your trouble? You're just too nice. Still, we'll work something out, don't you worry.'

There's still Ryan. Joan pauses in front of him.

'What are you going to do then, Ryan?' she says.

Ryan shrugs, looking miserable, hunched into his anorak.

'We'll have to leave him out,' says Cathy.

'No, we won't! Left-Outs don't do that, not to each other,' says Melvyn.

'Well, how can he do a play when he won't say a flipping word?' says Cathy.

'I know!' says Joan. 'Your play can be all in mime, Ryan. Do you know what mime is? You do it all the time, actually. You act things out without speaking. Clowns do it. Like this.' Joan pulls a miserable face and makes her whole body droop.

She rubs her tummy desperately. Then she notices Cathy's half-eaten Kit-Kat. Joan's eyes sparkle. She darts forward, snatches the Kit-Kat, and pops it into her mouth. She munches and then gives a big chocolatey smile, whirling round happily, patting her tummy.

'You greedy guts! That was *my* Kit-Kat,' says Cathy, indignantly.

But Ryan is smiling. He nods at Joan and gives her the thumbs-up sign.

'There,' says Joan. 'Now we're all doing a play. And we'll join them all up together and have one huge enormous incredible demonic drama.'

Seven

The Left-Outs spend every spare second rehearsing. Not *The Pied Piper*. They slouch through their rat roles, crashing and colliding in their special rat dance, devised by Miss Banks. She gets so cross with them, she makes them sit cross-legged with their hands on their heads like naughty five-year-olds.

Miss Morpeth is actually impressed by their costumes. Joan has worked wonders with their masks and they've rustled up enough leotards, dark T-shirts and shorts between them to clothe each rat. Joan's even managed to talk Tich into wearing *two* pairs of tights, one pair on his legs and the other twisted into a long tail. Finding eighteen pairs of tights was a bit of a problem, as not all the mothers could produce old unwanted pairs at the drop of a hat. Both Joan's Mum and Jackie are going to get a shock when they go looking in their underwear drawers.

It's important that they all have impressive costumes for the Demon play. The Left-Outs get together and act it out before school, at play-times, in the dinner hour. Even though they don't act in costume, they still attract an audience. Janice and Anita watch Joan give a particularly ferocious performance of Morgaslurp and pull silly faces.

'What are you mucking about like that for, Fatty? That bit's not in the play.'

'You buzz off and mind your own business,' says Joan.

Like a true professional, she carries on performing, in spite of the heckling. In fact she's spurred on to new heights of venom and violence, rushing round baring her teeth, pretending to take such savage bites that Janice and Anita get worried.

'If you try and bite me like that in the play I'm telling Miss Morpeth,' says Janice.

'She's completely nuts,' says Anita. 'They're all nuts. And it's mad, them doing all this rehearsing in the playground. It isn't getting them anywhere. They're still hopeless when we have a proper rehearsal of *The Pied Piper*.'

'Ah, but this isn't *The Pied*—' Dawn starts to say, but Morgaslurp's claws clamp over her mouth before she can say any more.

'Shut *up*, Dawn,' she hisses.

It's no use. They're going to have to try to find somewhere private to rehearse.

'I suppose you can all come back to tea with me and we can rehearse at my place,' says Joan, but even she is doubtful whether this is a good idea.

Mum is happy to welcome one friend home to tea. Or even two or three. But eight might be a bit much. And the new flat is so small, there's scarcely room for Joan and Jackie and Mum. It's not at all the right venue for a long, action-packed drama with a large and lively cast.

'What about you, Melvyn? You live in a big house. Can't we all go round to your place?' Joan asks.

'My mum's a bit funny about things like sticky fingers on the glass table top and scuff marks on the carpet,' says Melvyn gloomily. 'You'd all have to bring your slippers and we wouldn't be allowed to rush about in case we knocked over the ornaments.'

'We haven't *got* a proper carpet. Or ornaments,' says Cathy. 'We did have, but my little brothers keep spoiling and breaking everything. You can come back to my place but we'd never hear ourselves speak because someone's always yelling and the telly's always on full blast.'

'We're not allowed to have people back, are we, Pete?' says Louise.

'There's not enough room,' says Pete. 'There's not even enough room for us.'

'You can all come back to the squat with me,' says Summer, beaming at them. 'We can use any of the rooms.'

'My mum won't let me go round to your place,' says Dawn. 'She says you're all hippies and she's scared I'll catch something.'

'You'll catch something from me if you don't shut up, Dawn,' says Joan. 'Anyway, we need somewhere bigger than a room full of furniture. Somewhere bare. And private. Where we can really perform. You know. A *stage*.' And then she smiles.

The next time Miss Morpeth asks the Left-Outs to rehearse their rat roles in the classroom, they give a spectacularly bad performance, even by their standards. Miss Morpeth sits with her head in her hands, quietly moaning.

'What am I going to do with you?' she says. 'I don't understand it. Rory's word-perfect already—*and* he's learnt a very complicated tune to play on his recorder. Billy's stopped being boisterous and is giving a very creditable performance as the Mayor. Michael is wringing our hearts being the poor little crippled boy. All the townsfolk of Hamelin are very convincing and the children are delightful—and they do their lovely little skipping dance. But you rats! You're just running amok and spoiling everything.'

'I think we need a few more rehearsals, Miss Morpeth,' says Joan, earnestly. 'I'm sure we'll improve with a bit of practice.'

'Your performance certainly couldn't get any worse,' says Miss Morpeth. 'But I can't ask poor Miss Banks to try again with you. You were so silly and naughty with her, I'm thoroughly ashamed of you. And I'm much too busy myself to keep going through your parts with you.'

'Oh, I appreciate that, Miss Morpeth. No, what I mean is, can't we rats get together in the dinner hour—and use the proper stage in the Hall? I'm sure we wouldn't keep bumping into each other then. And if there was no-one staring at us, I'm sure we'd stop messing about and do it properly. Please, Miss Morpeth.'

'I know you, Joan Morgan. You're up to some mischief. You know perfectly well you're not allowed indoors in the dinner hour—and I can't possibly give up my precious time to supervise you.'

'We'll supervise ourselves. Don't worry. Miss Morpeth. We'll be as quiet as mice. Well, rats,' says Joan.

Normally Miss Morpeth would never give in. But she's tired out and very worried about *The Pied Piper*. The performance is in two weeks' time, half the costumes still aren't ready and she doesn't know what she's going to do about scenery or programmes and these wretched rats are proving such a problem . . .

'Oh, very well, Joan. You may rehearse on the stage this lunchtime. But I shall keep popping in to see that you're behaving. And I'm warning you, if I catch any of you up to any nonsense—particularly *you*, Joan—you will be in Very Serious Trouble. Do you understand?'

So the Left-Outs have their very own stage at dinner time. Miss Morpeth does indeed pop in and out. She sees what she thinks are nine unusually animated rats leaping around in a lively manner. She nods, looking surprised, and goes about her business.

Joan doesn't bother to beg for permission the next day. Or the next, or the next. The Left-Outs rush to the stage the moment the bell goes. They eat packed lunches during their performance. They forget all about *The Pied Piper* and their boring rat routine. They involve themselves in their own Demon play. They don't bother with saying the same words all the time. Joan is the only one who's actually written her play out in full, and she keeps getting new ideas for Morgaslurp anyway. The others tell their ideas too, and then they act it out, making it up as they go along. Sometimes they bicker a bit, arguing over parts. Sometimes they fool around. But there are other times when they all get so involved that it's as if it's all real and when the bell jangles for the start of afternoon school they all blink at each other in bewilderment.

'Blooming bell,' says Joan. 'Just as we were really getting cracking. If only we had enough time to give a proper performance, all the way through without a hitch.' She broods for a few moments. 'Of course, we can't really call it a performance, not without an audience. Wouldn't it be wonderful if we could stage our play and perform it to all the others?'

'We'd never be allowed,' says Melvyn.

'You're such a pessimist, Melvyn,' says Joan. 'You know we must really work hard at our play tomorrow, start to polish it up a bit. Then, when it's really, truly professional, we'll maybe ask Miss Morpeth if we can perform it properly, in front of the others. I bet she'd be so impressed she'd drop that boring old *Pied Piper* like a shot and put on our play instead. An then at the end, amidst the tumultuous applause, I'd come on and take a bow, because I'm the Chief Writer and Originator of the entire project and the Artistic Director and the Lead Actor and—'

'And Number One Bighead,' Cathy interrupts.

'You aren't half batty, Joan. Of course we'll never be able to perform our play.'

'Do you want to bet on it?' asks Joan.

But the Left-Outs aren't able to rehearse their Demon play the next lunchtime. Miss Morpeth decides that it's time for a first dress rehearsal of *The Pied Piper*. The Headmaster lets them have the Hall all morning. They need it. The rehearsal goes right through the lunch hour too.

Everything goes wrong. Rory suddenly forgets his lines and sqwawks hideously on his recorder. The Mayor and his Corporation seem inhibited by their robes and mumble in a monotone. The townswomen become self-conscious and suffer repeated attacks of the giggles. The children of Hamelin trip over their ropes in the skipping dance and the little crippled boy keeps forgetting to limp. And the rats give an excruciatingly awful performance. The Left-Outs have been so involved in their own play that they've forgotten the little they learnt for their parts in *The Pied Piper*. They either stand still looking stupid or rush about like maniacs, bumping into each other.

'I thought you'd been busy rehearsing!' Miss Morpeth shouts, furiously. 'This is ridiculous! And the performance is *next week*. The whole school is coming—*and* the parents. Coming to watch a positive fiasco!' Her voice cracks in her despair. She swallows, gasps, and struggles for composure. 'We'd better run through it once more. Come along. Please pull yourselves together. Try your hardest.'

The class tries—though some certainly try harder than others. Miss Morpeth shouts continuously. By the time they reach the end of the play it's nearly three o'clock and Miss Morpeth has lost her voice altogether.

'We'll just have to try again on Monday,' she whispers, painfully. 'Now. What am I going to do with you until the bell goes? How can I take a lesson when I can't even talk?'

Joan suddenly bobs up, her eyes glittering.

'Poor Miss Morpeth. Why don't you send someone to get you a cup of tea from the drinks dispenser? It wouldn't half help your poor sore throat. Why don't you sit down and relax? And all the cast with big parts, they can sit down too. Me and my fellow rats, we'll entertain you. We have a play of our own. We'll perform it for you.'

'I think I've seen too many performances already,' Miss Morpeth whispers faintly, but she can't summon enough energy to forbid it outright. She sits back, with the proffered cup of tea. The children sprawl on the Hall floor, exhausted too.

'Come on, then,' Joan hisses to the Left-Outs. 'It's our big chance!'

'Oh, Joan! I wish you hadn't! I can't act, not in front of all the others,' Melvyn squeaks.

'Of course you can!' says Joan, sternly.

'They'll all laugh at us,' says Cathy.

'Yeah, the boys will take the mick something awful,' says Tich.

'Then we'll bash them up afterwards,' says Joan. 'For goodness sake! This is our big chance. What's *up* with you? I'm the leader and I command you to get up on the stage and act our play!'

They still waver. Then Melvyn sighs.

'I suppose all Left-Outs have to stick up for each other. And this play thing does mean an awful lot to Joan,' he says.

'It means an awful lot to all of us!' Joan insists. 'Come on!'

But once she's up on the stage even Joan begins to have her doubts. There's all the class looking up at her, whispering and nudging each other. She turns her back on them and takes several deep breaths.

'Right,' she whispers. 'This is our big chance. Everyone thinks we're going to make complete fools of ourselves. But we're going to show them. We're the Left-Outs—and this is our own super-special play. So let's start it. You know, the way we always begin.'

Joan lies down on the stage. The other Left-Outs lie down too and close their eyes.

'This is such a boring play that even the cast have gone to sleep,' Janice giggles.

'It's not a bit boring, honestly. You'll really like it,' Dawn hisses.

'Sh!' says Joan, poking her. 'You're here to act, not to chat up the audience.'

There is silence. Then Joan pretends to be a clock, striking nine loud chimes. She stretches and stands up.

'Nine chimes! It will be daytime in the world above. Waken, my fellow Demons,' she calls, in

Morgaslurp's harsh, cackling voice.

The other Left-Outs stretch and stand. They hold hands and then circle slowly as they proclaim Joan's special Demon chant:

> 'Hark, in our dark,
> Here we stand, hand in hand,
> Nine Demons of hell
> Who wish no-one well,
> About to enter your life
> And bring hassle and strife,
> So beware of our bile,
> Our cunning and guile.
> We fume as we fly,
> Watch out, or you'll die!'

They whirl faster and faster in the circle now, stamping and shouting, and then Joan screams, 'Let us wreak havoc!' They break hands and whirl round separately, weaving in and out of each other, their masks unmistakably demonic now. There's no scuttling or squeaky rattiness about any of them. They are fearsome devils. When Joan suddenly lunges towards the audience with a shriek of 'Beware!' several children recoil in panic.

It is Joan's big moment now, her Morgaslurp drama. She dances by herself, swooping around the stage, while the other Left-Outs remove their masks. They sit cross-legged, reciting pretend lessons, while Dawn marches around them, one hand on her hip, looking very stern. During their many rehearsals they have actually called Dawn Miss Morpeth but Joan senses this might not be wise in an actual performance with Miss Morpeth herself as part of the audience. She calls her Miss Dawn instead and plagues her thoroughly, playing silly tricks on her and calling her mildly rude names (nowhere near as inventively rude as some of the names in previous rehearsals). In spite of all these precautions Joan can't help worrying a little when she glances at Miss Morpeth, and once or twice she loses concentration and forgets her lines.

It's a relief when the schoolroom scene is over and Morgaslurp flies to the lair of the disgusting Dizzylizzie (Summer being wonderfully spidery) who has Fatheramous at her mercy. Tich is a very short Fatheramous. He only comes up to Morgaslurp's shoulders but it can't be helped. Morgaslurp frees him from Dizzylizzie's loathsome stickiness and then wraps her up in her own web to writhe in agony. Summer writhes very impressively, rolling around the stage and wildly contorting her arms and legs.

Then it's Summer's turn to be the star, as the Demon Winter. She tosses all her long hair over her face and puts her mask on the back of her head so it looks horribly as if her head is twisted back to front. She does an effective Winter dance, very authoritarian, marching up and down with little clipped steps, prodding the other Left-Outs with a ruler to make them stand upright. She doesn't really have any lines to say because she never got round to writing them, but she dances around so inventively that doesn't matter. She ends up marching everyone offstage and then standing alone, looking all about her. There is no-one left to command so she takes control of herself, frog-marching herself away.

Cathy and Tich have combined their plays. Cathykiller and Lofty are two violent Demons with an entire arsenal of weapons at their disposal. They shoot indiscriminately, making loud realistic machine gun noises and soon the stage is littered with dead bodies. Then Cathykiller and Lofty have a final desperate shoot-out with each other and experience prolonged and gruesome deaths.

Louise and Pete emerge from the pile of dead bodies as Rubbish-Tip Demons. They sweep all the bodies up and pick the pockets with glee. They find a door key in Melvyn's pocket—'Don't lose it, eh, or my mother will go spare,' Melvyn whispers anxiously—and wander around, trying the key in many locks.

'We've tried every lock in the land,' says Louise.

'Every lock but one,' says Pete. 'We haven't tried the Palace.'

So they pretend to go to the Palace and of course the key fits and the two Demons luxuriate in the splendour, running the golden hot water taps and dancing wildly round the spacious rooms. They eventually subside and start to work their way through a seven-course meal served by invisible servants. Whilst they are busy munching, Melvyn bobs up at the front of the stage.

'I'm the Demon Imp, small and sinister and savage,' he hisses, making all the 'esses' positively sizzle in his mouth.

But then Billy says loudly, 'Who does Smelly Melly think he is, eh?'

Poor Melvyn stops and stutters, hanging his head.

'You're *not* Smelly Melly. You're the Demon Imp,' Joan whispers, as she rushes back on stage. She stomps around doing a gorilla walk, arms swinging, legs apart, a wonderfully gormless expression on her face.

'I'm Bully Billy,' she announces, swaggering about, raising a great laugh and cheer from her audience.

'And I'm the Demon Imp,' says Melvyn, with renewed confidence, and he darts about the stage, tweaking Billy's nose, tripping him over, even kicking him in the seat of the pants, while Bully Billy lumbers about helplessly, far too slow and stupid to stop him.

Then it's Dawn's turn and she capers about, tossing her head and kicking up her legs.

'Hello, everybody,' she says, and puts her hand behind her ear.

'Hello, Dawn!' call the rest of the class.

'Yes, I'm funny, friendly, Demon-Dawn, here to make you all laugh,' she says, jumping up and down, doing her own version of the Highland Fling. She flings a little too enthusiastically and trips over her own feet. She sends herself sprawling and lands on her bottom, looking very surprised.

'Just bow and act like it's part of the show,' Joan whispers. 'Now it's you, Ryan. Go on. Don't be scared. Just mime any old thing.'

They've never got around to rehearsing Ryan's part. There's never been time before, because they've been so involved with the rest of the play. Ryan's never seemed to mind. But he's minding now. His eyes peep out from behind his mask, plainly terrified. He crouches down in a corner of the stage, trying to hide his head.

'Oh dear,' says Joan. She waits a moment, and then sidles up to Ryan, to try to reassure him. When he hears her footsteps, he scuttles away from her, but he gives a little wink as he goes. Joan catches on. He's only acting. This is all part of his play. So she pretends to chase after him while he dodges this way and that. The other Left-Outs join in the chase. The chase goes on for a long time. Joan isn't sure what should happen next. Does Ryan want them to catch him or not?

'What do we do now?' she hisses at him.

Ryan's mask moves. He's obviously mouthing the words, but Joan can't see behind the cardboard.

'I can't see your lips,' she hisses. 'Ryan! Help us! Shall we catch you?'

Ryan nods.

So Joan pounces and she and the other Left-Outs capture Ryan, although he struggles very effectively.

'Now what?' Joan hisses. 'Is that it? Are you finished now?'

Ryan shakes his head.

'Well, what do you want us to do? Oh Ryan, come on, you'll have to *tell* us.'

There's a pause. And then . . . 'Put me in a cage,'

someone whispers in a very small voice. 'Leave me alone. Then put on your Demon masks. Come back. You're my Demon friends and you rescue me from the cage and we all dance round together.'

'Ryan's talking!' says Melvyn.

'Well, come on. Don't let's stand here like lemons. Let's act it out,' Joan hisses.

So they do exactly that. They lock Ryan in a pretend cage, making great play of banging the gate and locking it up with Melvyn's key. Then they go away, but come creeping back in their Demon masks. Ryan jumps for joy when he sees them, reaching out through the bars of the cage to hold hands with them. Joan is prepared to do a great deal of miming with spare keys, but Tich gets there first by pretending to seize the bars of the cage and simply ripping them apart. Ryan leaps out and they all dance round him.

They perform their circle dance, fast and furious, and then when they're all getting out of breath Joan chimes like a clock and chants:

'Now we must get back to Hell.
We've wreaked havoc very well.'
Then she swoops them all off the stage.

There's a silence from the audience. Joan sighs impatiently.

'It's the end,' she calls. 'You can clap now.'

And at last they do start clapping.

Eight

Miss Morpeth eases herself to her feet.

'Well, well, well,' she says, huskily. 'So this is what you've been up to.'

'It's a great play, isn't it, Miss Morpeth,' says Joan. 'Of course, it needs a bit more polishing, and there are some bits that went a bit wonky. But on the whole it is good, isn't it? I wrote all the Morgaslurp bit and directed the whole thing.'

'I rather thought you did,' says Miss Morpeth.

'So what do you think about us giving a proper performance to the whole school? And maybe the parents too?' Joan asks, eagerly. 'Maybe we could have several performances. If we had them in the evening we could sell tickets to the general public and—'

'Joan! No. I don't think that would be a good idea at all,' says Miss Morpeth, and although her voice is hoarse, it is also firm.

'But *why?*' Joan says, devastated.

'Your play is too—unusual.'

'You mean it's original? Well, that's a good thing, isn't it?'

'And it's too disjointed.'

'Yes, well, that's because we all wrote bits of it. But I could always do some more joining up bits.

We could have another scene in the Demons' cave of hell fire.'

'That's another point, Joan,' says Miss Morpeth. 'Some people might find the idea of a play about wicked demons rather offensive.'

'Oh, but Miss Morpeth, look at the things you see on the television. And some of the videos you can get, they show you the most disgusting things.'

'I don't wish to know about them, thank you. Just take my word for it, Joan. Your play is not suitable.'

'So it's all been a waste of time,' Joan says, sulkily.

'No, it hasn't,' says Miss Morpeth. She walks up the steps onto the stage. 'I think you've all been very contrary, putting so much obvious effort into this play and not trying at all with *The Pied Piper*. However, you've shown me that you *can* all act. And so I'm going to expect far more from you when we come to perform *The Pied Piper*.'

'But Miss Morpeth, it's so boring,' says Joan, still sulking.

Melvyn gives her a nudge to shut her up, but nothing will keep her quiet now.

'Who could possibly get excited about playing a silly old rat?' says Joan. 'Even Sir Laurence Olivier would barely deign to twitch a whisker.'

'Joan, will you stop arguing with me!' Miss Morpeth tries to shout. She swallows several times and continues in a whisper. 'Why can't you act your rat part the way you did your Demon?'

'You mean make my rat like Morgaslurp?'

'Exactly! You can make him as cross and wicked and sly and cunning as you like. You can all act out your Demon personalities and really bring the rats to life. Life, Cathy and Tich, not death. You were very inventive but much too bloodthirsty. You can both be cruel and violent rats, but within reason. You can maybe have a fight with each other—but we can't have any maiming or killing.

'Now, Dawn, you made a delightful comical Demon. You can certainly make your rat performance as funny as you can. Well done, dear, you've really tried hard. Summer, you're obviously a splendid natural actress—and your dancing is very impressive. If you can do a marching dance for your rat the way you did for your Demon I think it will prove very effective. And you must be a fierce little impish rat, Melvyn. Once you gained confidence you were magnificent. Louise and Peter, I really enjoyed your double act. We could certainly incorporate that idea into *The Pied Piper*. Ryan, I was delighted by your performance. You mimed so expressively. Yes, you've all tried very hard.' Miss Morpeth pauses. 'Especially you, Joan. Your play is a splendid success, even if it isn't quite suitable for public performance. You're obviously brimming with talent—even though you're such a trial to teach!'

Joan goes running home in triumph that afternoon. When Jackie gets back from school she tells her all about her hour of glory. When Mum gets back from work she tells her too, embellishing the details.

'I wish you could have seen me, Mum,' says Joan. 'Still, you will come to *The Pied Piper* on Friday afternoon, won't you?'

'Oh, Joan. You know I'd love to come, but I honestly don't see how I can get off. We've got such a lot of work at the moment. And my boss made such a fuss when I had to stay off the other week for the plumber. Incidentally Joan, I thought you were meant to be handing over your pocket money?'

'Don't change the subject, Mum! It's going to be horrible with no-one specially watching me. Melvyn's mum is coming.'

'Maybe she doesn't work. I do. But Joan, I know who would like to come and see you. Dad.'

'I don't want *him* to come,' says Joan. 'Anyway, he works too.'

'Yes, but his hours are more flexible. I'm sure he could get away. And he's been missing you so much.'

'Well, I haven't been missing him one little bit,' Joan lies.

'That's silly, Joan. Look. Your Dad and I—we don't love each other any more. But we both love you. And you and Dad, you were always so close.'

'He's close to that dumb Dizzylizzie now,' Joan mumbles.

'Don't call her that,' says Mum, but she gives a little giggle. 'OK. He's got this girlfriend. But you've got all your friends, Joan.'

Joan considers. She really has got friends now. Melvyn's her best friend. And then Cathy isn't really so bad when you get to know her. Or Louise and Pete. Tich is good fun. She likes Summer. She's getting surprisingly fond of Dawn. And Ryan might prove a really special friend too.

'OK,' says Joan. 'Dad can be friends with Dizzylizzie. But *I* don't have to be friends with her too, do I?'

'Well,' says Mum. 'That might take a bit of time.'

'Like forever,' says Joan. But then she smiles. 'Maybe I'll phone Dad, eh?'

Dad is delighted to hear from her. Joan shows off about her Demon play, outlining part of the plot and acting it out over the telephone. She invites Dad to the performance of *The Pied Piper* on Friday afternoon and he's thrilled.

'Of course, there's only one seat available per child. You can't bring anyone else with you,' says Joan.

'I understand,' says Dad. 'Now. What about this Sunday, Joan? Are you free?'

'I . . . could be,' says Joan. 'How about just you and me going to that nice pub for lunch and then the children's zoo and then we could maybe go back to your flat, just you and me, right, and we could have tea together and I could maybe act out a bit of my play for you so you can actually see it in person.'

There's a little pause. 'What about Jackie?' says Dad.

'Oh, she's off with her boring Mick again. They're a sort of couple now.'

'Ah. Well. Listen, Joan. We'll go to the pub. We'll go to the zoo. And I'd like more than anything for you to come back to the flat for tea. But Lizzie will be there too. Because we're a sort of couple too, you see. It's her home as well as mine.'

Joan goes out with Dad on Sunday. She's decided she's going to be very cool and composed but when she sees him she's suddenly so pleased, she throws her arms round his neck and they have a big hug that lasts for a very long time. Then they go off in Dad's car and Joan tells him about her Demon play yet again (still not mentioning two of the minor characters) and then she tells him about *The Pied Piper* and although she doesn't divulge any specific information about the Left-Outs, she tells him all about her new friends too.

They have lunch in the pub (chicken supreme and double-choc gateau) and an ice-cream in Battersea Park.

'Coming back to the flat for tea?' Dad says, trying hard to sound casual.

'Well, I'm a bit full up now,' says Joan.

'OK,' says Dad, but he looks so upset she can't bear it.

'But I could sort of pop in. Just for five minutes.'

Lizzie's been more laid back about tea this time. But there's a special iced sponge cake studded with Smarties. Red and yellow Smarties in the shape of a long thin man—and black and brown Smarties all round the edge.

'A Pied Piper cake,' says Lizzie. 'And those are the rats.'

92

'Mmm,' says Joan.

'I got some marzipan and I tried to make a rat or two out of that, but I can't do that sort of modelling.'

'Have you still got the marzipan?' asks Joan.

'Yes, it's in the fridge.'

'Can I have a go? I'm quite good at that sort of thing,' says Joan.

Lizzie brings out a great big lump of yellow marzipan. They all sit round having a go. Lizzie can only manage odd little blobs. Dad makes a very lumpy Pied Piper, but he keels over in all directions, and they haven't got any red colouring so he's not properly pied. It takes Joan a little while to get used to the marzipan. It's much softer and oozier than Plasticine. But when she gets the hang of it, she make a very credible-looking rat, with a sharp nose and a long tail.

'That's very good, Joan,' says Lizzie.

'It's just a little knack I have,' says Joan. 'Can I make some more? Eight more?'

'Make as many as you like. And have some cake while you're working,' says Lizzie.

'OK,' says Joan.

She ends up having several slices of cake, munching her way through the black and brown Smarties. She makes nine little marzipan rats and Lizzie finds her a box to put them in, assuring her that marzipan keeps for quite a while.

'Thanks,' says Joan, as she says goodbye.

She's still not friends with Lizzie, of course. But perhaps they're no longer enemies.

The Left-Outs have no opportunity to be Left-Outs all week. They are forced to join in like mad with the rest of the class during endless rehearsals of *The Pied Piper*. Many things still go wrong during these rehearsals—but the rats' performance is much improved. They do their own demon circle dance, but crouched over, with their hands curled into paws. Joan finds it really works, pretending to be a Morgaslurp demonic rat. She is almost beginning to enjoy herself.

She wakes up very early on Friday morning, too excited to sleep any more. Today's the big performance. She gets up and rushes around getting dressed, whistling the tune Rory plays on his recorder. Jackie puts her head out from her duvet and complains bitterly but later, at breakfast, she gives Joan a sudden hug.

'Good luck with your play, Joanie. I bet you'll be the best rat ever,' she says.

And Mum's even got her a good luck card, with some little mice eating their way through a huge wedge of cheese.

'They were the nearest I could get to rats,' says Mum. 'I do wish I could see your performance, darling.'

'Tell you what, Mum. I'll act out my bit for you this evening,' says Joan.

She rushes off to school, carefully carrying the cardboard box of marzipan rats. She gives one to each of the Left-Outs as a good luck gift.

They're all thrilled, though Cathy says she doesn't like marzipan.

94

'Well I do, so give it straight back and I'll eat yours too,' says Joan.

'No,' says Cathy, holding it away from her. 'No, I like the way it looks. I'm going to keep it on the window sill as an ornament.'

'I'm eating mine,' says Dawn, biting off its head. 'Yum yum. I didn't know rats tasted so delicious.'

The others eat theirs too, except for Melvyn.

'I'm going to keep it for a bit, as a souvenir,' he says.

He puts the rat on his desk top.

Billy and Mike come along and peer at it.

'Oh, what's this? Is it your little toy, Smelly Melly?' says Billy, and he clenches his fist above the marzipan rat.

'You flatten that and I'll flatten you,' Joan growls.

'It's OK, Joan. Silly Billy and Mikey Wikey must have their little game,' says Melvyn.

'Who do you think you are, Smelly Melly, calling us names? When you getting into your costumes, eh? He looks a right twit in his tights, doesn't he, Mike?'

'You look just as twitty in your Mayor's gown,' says Melvyn. 'At least I'm not wearing a dress.'

'It isn't a dress!' says Billy, furiously.

'Yeah, we girls are really envious of that brocade, Billy. And that big necklace too,' says Joan.

'It's a Mayor's chain—not a flipping necklace,' says Billy, stomping off. Mike follows.

Joan and Melvyn grin at each other.

'Get you, sticking up for yourself,' says Joan.

'Well. I just looked at that little marzipan rat. And I thought, that's what I'm like. A wee mousy creature just waiting to get thumped. So I tried talking back to them. And it worked!'

'Great. Though don't get too carried away. Sometimes you can answer back and you *still* get thumped,' says Joan.

They rehearse all morning. Then, after lunch, they start getting into their costumes and Miss Morpeth rushes round putting on everyone's make-up—apart from the Left-Outs who have their masks. Joan and Melvyn titter considerably when Billy and Mike are made up. When they're all ready they go over to the Hall. Miss Morpeth tries to settle them all quietly behind the stage.

'Good luck,' she says. She gives them a surprising smile. It's very odd seeing her without her usual stern expression. 'Just relax and enjoy performing the play,' she says. 'I'm very proud of all of you. I know you'll do well.'

They don't let her down. Rory remembers all his words and plays his recorder without a single sqwawk. Billy's performance is a little subdued at first, because he looks so self-conscious in his make-up and spendid gown and chains, but he soon livens up. All the citizens of Hamelin gossip animatedly and the children skip in step. The little crippled boy limps very pathetically and hangs his head, so that some of the parents watching go 'Aaaaah!' in sympathy.

But guess who are the star performers. The rats!

96

Melvyn scampers cheekily about the stage, stalking the Mayor, pretending to bite his bottom. Cathy hides behind corners and jumps out at everyone with a ferocious squeak. Louise and Pete scuttle together, keeping perfect time with each other. Tich jumps about everywhere, waving his paws. Every so often he gets carried away and gives people thumps in an un-ratlike manner, but the parents roar with laughter at his antics. They laugh delightedly at Dawn, too, as she capers about, knocking everything over and creating general havoc. Summer struts about the stage, almost frighteningly sinister. Ryan mimes being caught in a rat trap. He actually give a small squeak as he's caught. But then Joan organizes all the other rats to come to help him and he limps free.

Joan does a little dance of triumph. She bounces about the stage, the biggest, fiercest, funniest rat of all. She fights and kills and bites and eats and licks and tears and spoils, leaping about with demonic glee. She tugs the robes of the Mayor and his Corporation. She squeaks in the faces of all the gossipping townswomen—and even gnaws the shoe of one of them!

When Rory, as the Pied Piper, starts playing his magic music, Joan is instantly suspicious and covers her ears with her paws. But after a while, even she can't resist and is charmed away against her will, though she tries hard to clutch at the horrible rat trap, knowing that's her only hope. But she's broken the spring rescuing Ryan, and it can't trap her.

She's borne away by the magic music, squeaking and shrieking.

'Well done, Joan!' Miss Morpeth hisses at her. 'That was brilliantly inventive.'

Joan joins the rest of the Left-Outs, glowing.

'You were all great!' she says. 'Here, I forgot to look for Dad! I got so involved being my Morgaslurp Ratty. I was going to give Dad a special wave too—and now it's too late.'

But it's not too late. At the end of the play Miss Morpeth tells all the cast to go on stage to take a bow. So Joan joins the others—and spots Dad at once this time. He's sitting right at the front, amongst all the mothers and toddler brothers and sisters, and he's smiling and waving and clapping for all he's worth.

Miss Morpeth instructs Billy to take a special bow as the Mayor, then the little crippled boy, and then the Pied Piper. They all three hold hands, bowing.

'What about the fat rat?' shouts someone in the audience.

'Yes! Take a bow, fat rat!' shouts someone else.

'My name's *Joan*,' says Joan indignantly, but she takes a bow and everyone claps and cheers.

BIG IGGY

Kaye Umansky

When large Lizzy decides it's time she had a bit of peace and quiet, Big Iggy – the smallest dragon – and his brothers all take off into the big wide world. But Big Iggy's first flight ends with a crash landing into a tree – and a huge adventure.

WITCHES IN STITCHES

Kaye Umansky

Your very own monster magazine! Jokes, interviews, competitions, quizzes, health and beauty, songs, poems, lonely hearts, horrorscopes, special offers – it's packed with original and totally unexpected fun.

BAGTHORPES LIBERATED

Helen Cresswell

In the seventh book about the eccentric Bagthorpe family, Mrs Bagthorpe is determined to liberate the female members of the household from domestic drudgery and sets out to rally support for her radical views. But a string of hilarious incidents proves all too clearly that if there is one thing Mrs Bagthorpe can never e, it's liberated.

FIT WIT!

ed. Biddy Baxter

To celebrate the National Health Service's 40th birthday, BBC television's *Blue Peter* held a cartoon competition and received not hundreds ... but thousands of entries. The funniest and most original have been chosen for *Fit Wit!* With this hilarious book in your hands, hospitals, doctors and nurses will never seem the same again.

AWFUL ANNIE STORIES

J. B. Simpson

When dreary Aunt Binkie comes to stay, Annie unexpectedly becomes her closest ally – and all because of a tiny stray terrier called Percy. Then muddle-headed Annie borrows a wonder machine called Nippy Numbers and promptly loses it. Her desperate attempts to recover it lead her through a series of breath-taking adventures.

NOW THEN, CHARLIE ROBINSON

Sylvia Woods

Charlie Robinson is always full of ideas, whether he's trying to help liven up a maths lesson, solve the mystery of noises up a chimney or turn the Nativity Play into a really special event. His exploits at home, at school and out and about in the village make very entertaining reading.

SON OF A GUN
Janet and Allan Ahlberg

A galloping, riotous wild west farce in which the plot thickens with every page until a combined force of Indians, US cavalry, old-timers, dancing-girls and the 8-year-old hero are racing to the rescue of a mother and baby, besieged in their cabin by two incompetent bandits called Slocum. As one of the Slocums says, 'Cavalry *and* Indians? Where's the fairness in that?'

HENRY AND RIBSY
Beverly Cleary

Henry's dream is to go fishing with his father. He can just see himself sitting in a boat, reeling in an enormous salmon. Mr Huggins has promised he will take Henry fishing on one condition: that he keeps Ribsy out of trouble and does not let him annoy the neighbours, especially Mr Grumble next door. The trouble is, keeping a dog like Ribsy under control isn't that easy!

WILL THE REAL GERTRUDE HOLLINGS PLEASE STAND UP?
Sheila Greenwald

Gertrude is in a bad way. She's a bit slow at school but everyone thinks she's dumb and her teachers call her 'Learning Disabled' behind her back. As if this isn't enough, her parents go off on a business trip leaving her with her aunt and uncle and her obnoxious cousin, Albert — a 'superachiever'. Gertrude is determined to win Perfect Prize-Winning Albert's respect by whatever means it takes . . .

MR BROWSER AND THE SPACE MAGGOTS
Philip Curtis

When it rains every playtime for a month and the school field
turns brown, Mr Browser and Class 8 of Chivvy Chase School
begin to suspect that something odd is happening. But the local
Nature Reserve Warden has mysteriously disappeared, leaving
behind him strange messages about Space Maggots. Is there anything Selwyn, Anna and Spiky can do to foil the Space Maggots' devilish plan?

WELL, WELL, WELL
Dr Peter Rowan

Find out what your body can (and can't) do; how its many parts
work together to keep you healthy; what happens when things
go wrong and who and what can make you better. Dr Pete
gives some top tips on how to keep yourself (and others) fit, as
well as some breath-taking facts about your body which will
amaze and amuse you.

THE GREAT PUFFIN JOKE DIRECTORY
Brough Girling

No great directory could start without an aardvark joke. Use
this directory to find out what Humpty did with his hat, how to
start a jelly race and what the vampire's favourite soup is . . .
Packed with alphabetical fun to keep you and your friends giggling for years, this is the world's funniest A–Z of jokes.

TALES FROM THE SHOP THAT NEVER SHUTS

Martin Waddell

McGlone lives at the Shop that Never Shuts, and Flash and Buster Cook are in McGlone's Gang with wee Biddy O'Hare. In these five highly entertaining stories the Gang dig for Viking treasure, are frightened that a sea monster has eaten Biddy, discover that McGlone needs glasses, look after the Shop that Never Shuts on their own, and give Biddy a birthday party.

VERA PRATT AND THE BALD HEAD

Brough Girling

When Wally Pratt and his fanatic mechanic mother enter the Motorbike and Sidecar Grand Prix, nothing is really as it seems. Vera's old enemy, Captain Smoothy-Smythe, is up to his old tricks and suddenly Wally is kidnapped. Rescue him? She can't do that yet, she's got to win the Grand Prix first. Two minutes to go and Vera finds herself the ideal partner – a headmaster with no hair!

CRUMMY MUMMY AND ME

Anne Fine

How would you feel if your mother had royal-blue hair and wore lavender fishnet tights? It's not easy for Minna being the only sensible one in the family, even though she's used to her mum's weird clothes and eccentric behaviour. But then the whole family are a bit unusual, and their exploits make very entertaining and enjoyable reading.

SANTA'S DIARY
Shoo Rayner

What's life really like for Santa Claus as the build-up begins for Christmas. Meet him, his family, his reindeer and a host of other characters and read his extraordinary personal life story in this amazing never-before-published diary.

RUDOLPH'S CHRISTMAS FUN BOOK
Martyn Forrester

A Christmas activity book – sacks full of Christmas crosswords, quizzes, fax, puzzles, games, jokes and lots of fun things to do instead of watching the Christmas edition of Neighbours! This one will sleigh you (ho ho).

GOGGLE-EYES
Anne Fine

Kitty hated Gerald Faulkner from the moment she met him. What her mother saw in him she couldn't imagine. He was quite unlike her father and had nothing in common with any of them as far as she could see, and his goggling at her mother's legs really got on her nerves. But when 'Goggle-Eyes' left after a dramatic quarrel, Kitty was amazed to discover she missed him . . . A thoroughly entertaining, sensitive, sometimes serious but always very funny novel.